Gully's Travels
Tor Seidler
Pictures by Brock Cole

Author: Tor Seidler / Illustrator: Brock Cole

Publication Date: September 2008

Format: Hardcover

ISBN-13: 978-0-545-02506-5

ISBN-10: 0-545-02506-0

Retail Price: $16.95 US / $18.95 CAN

Ages: 8 and up

Grades: 3 and up

LC number: 2007936513

Length: 192 pages

Trim: 6 ¾″ x 8 ⅞″

Classification: Fiction

MICHAEL DI CAPUA BOOKS / SCHOLASTIC
557 Broadway, New York, New York 10012

Books by Tor Seidler

The Dulcimer Boy

Terpin

A Rat's Tale

The Tar Pit

The Wainscott Weasel

Mean Margaret

The Silent Spillbills

The Revenge of Randal Reese-Rat

Brothers Below Zero

Brainboy and the Deathmaster

Toes

Gully's Travels

Gully's Travels

GULLY'S TRAVELS

Tor Seidler
Pictures by Brock Cole

Michael di Capua Books
Scholastic

Contents

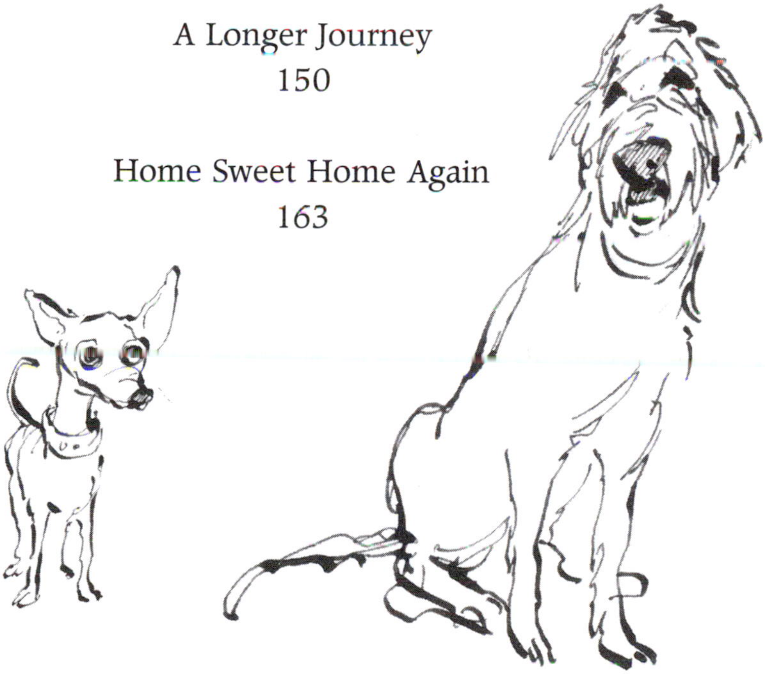

Gully's Travels

A New
Acquaintance

When Gulliver and Rodney first met, on a sunny Saturday in May, they didn't give each other the usual thorough sniffing. They simply stopped and eyed each other. Both were quite reserved.

Rodney was a couple of inches taller. He had a salt-and-pepper coat and a face even Gulliver found distinguished: long and square with thick eyebrows, a fine beard, and a mustache every bit as impressive as Gulliver's own.

"One of those German breeds?" Gulliver said.

"Schnauzer," said Rodney. "And you're Tibetan?"

"Lhasa apso," Gulliver said proudly. "Though I was born right here in New York City."

"As was I."

"Miniature?"

Rodney, who didn't like this term, frowned.

To redeem himself—and with luck get a compliment in return—Gulliver said, "Nice collar."

Contrary to common wisdom, dogs aren't color-blind. Gulliver could see perfectly well that the schnauzer's leather collar was a handsome forest green. But it paled in comparison with his salmon-pink one. Gulliver despised salmon (or any other fish) for dinner, but the color was irresistible. Furthermore, the collar was studded with pieces of turquoise set in silver.

Striking as the collar looked against Gulliver's honey coat, Rodney just lifted a thick eyebrow and said, "Yours is . . . Where on earth did you get it?"

Gulliver rose to his full eleven inches and flicked a look at the blond, goateed man holding his leash. "He brought it back for me from one of his trips."

"Ah."

Ah what? Gulliver wondered, getting a little hot under the aforementioned collar. Normally dogs were as impressed by his collar as they were by his pure breeding and fine intelligence. "You must be new to the neighborhood," he said, lifting his snout.

"Oh, we don't live around *here*." Rodney surveyed Washington Square Park as if it were a slum. "There's a food shop around the corner he likes."

The schnauzer indicated his leash holder, a man whose salt-and-pepper hair matched Rodney's coat. In his leash hand the man was also holding a bag.

"Is he a good cook?" Gulliver asked.

"Gourmet."

"As is mine. Does he give you scraps?"

"Of course."

"Mine, too."

"What's your usual?"

"Prime Premium."

"Really? Same here. What's your favorite flavor?"

"Beef and Liver Delight. You?"

"Chicken and Cheese Surprise. How often do you go to the groomer?"

"Once a month," Gulliver said, tossing a silken lock out of his eyes.

"Me, too."

"Groom-o-rama on Bank Street?"

"Oh, heavens, no. Ours is on the Upper East Side."

Gulliver, who wasn't used to dogs challenging his superiority, looked away coldly. They were in the corner of Washington Square Park where the outdoor chess tables are, and for a while he watched a pigeon debating the wisdom of dashing under one of the occupied tables for a piece of hot-dog bun. But in time his eyes returned warily to the schnauzer.

"*They* seem to be getting along," Rodney remarked.

In big cities like New York, human strangers usually ignore each other. But if they're walking dogs, even the most standoffish people will start chatting away. Topic number one is naturally the dogs themselves, but Gulliver's and Rodney's leash holders had already progressed to other things. They had a lot in common. Both were professors. Gulliver's owner, Professor Rattigan, taught English literature at nearby New York University, while Rodney's owner, Professor Moroni, taught modern art farther uptown, at Hunter College. Both men were single, Professor Rattigan having never married, Professor Moroni being divorced. Both were cultivated, both came from well-to-do families. Moreover, both men liked chess. In fact, the only reason Professor Moroni had detoured into the park was to check out the chess games.

They focused on a game being waged between an elderly Japanese man and a pallid, blue-eyed boy.

"The boy's trying to sucker him with his bishop," Professor Moroni whispered.

"Mm," Professor Rattigan whispered back. "Seems to be working, doesn't it?"

Eventually Professor Rattigan nodded at a vacant table and asked Professor Moroni if he would like to try a game sometime.

"Love to," Professor Moroni said.

"Tomorrow afternoon?"

"Fine. I'll bring a set."

"I'll bring a timer—unless you object."

"Not at all! If there's one thing I can't stand, it's people who agonize over their moves for fifteen minutes."

"I couldn't agree with you more. Shall we say two o'clock?"

"Providing it's not raining."

Dogs pick up only occasional scraps of human speech, but both Gulliver and Rodney noted the friendly way the men shook hands.

"It looks as if we may be seeing each other again," Rodney commented.

"Mm," Gulliver said. *"À bientôt."*

He was about to explain that this was the French way of saying "See you soon" when Rodney said:

"Gotten Grog."

Sunday in the Park
with Rodney

Gulliver and his professor lived just north of Washington Square at one of the most fashionable addresses in Manhattan: One Fifth Avenue. Their apartment occupied fully half of the seventeenth floor, and Gulliver considered it heaven. The faded rugs and brown leather sofas and chairs were as comfortable as they were tasteful. The antiques were of the highest quality. The paneling on the walls was of the finest oak. The windows, facing north, east, and west, were framed in dark, heavy drapes that reached all the way to the floor, creating ideal hiding places. And everywhere you looked, bookshelves burst with books that contained, Gulliver was quite sure, the wisdom of the entire world.

His professor's choice of footwear was reddish-brown, tasseled loafers, a half dozen pairs of which, all with a glossy shine, were lined up along a wall of the master bedroom. Beyond these was Gulliver's bed. It was so cozy, with its flowery chintz cushion, that he sometimes hated leaving it, but he always got up in the morning along with his professor. Loyalty is the hallmark of the well-bred dog—especially the Lhasa apso.

That next day, however, was Sunday, and on Sundays they slept in. And when his professor finally did get up, he didn't guzzle a cup of coffee, take him for a quick walk, then rush off to a class or his office. They took a leisurely stroll around the neighborhood, picked up the Sunday *Times*, and returned home for a real breakfast. As a treat his professor cooked two extra strips of bacon to mix in with Gulliver's morning half can of Prime Premium.

After breakfast, in the elegant, high-ceilinged living room, Professor Rattigan put on a German opera and sat reading the paper. Gulliver, curled up beside him on the sofa, hadn't had much use for newspapers since his housebreaking days, but opera was another matter. As a puppy he'd thought it sounded like sick cats wailing at the moon, but over time the Italian operas had grown on him, and now that he was a mature dog he even enjoyed the German ones.

Not today, though. Today he ground his canine teeth through all three discs. For although he could tell German from Italian, he couldn't understand a word of it. And *Gotten Grog,* he was convinced, was German.

Could that distinguished-looking Rodney be a more refined and sophisticated dog than he was?

At around one o'clock they went out again. As usual,
his professor didn't attach the leash till they stepped
from the elevator into the building's checkerboard marble lobby.

"Hey, Dr. Rattigan," said Carlos the doorman, opening the door for them. "Hey, Gully."

Distasteful as it was having his name shortened that way, Carlos was so cheerful that Gulliver never snarled at him.

He and his professor proceeded to a dog-friendly sandwich shop on Waverly Place. Gulliver prided himself on sitting politely under tables in restaurants and cafés without moving or making a peep, and today he got his usual reward: a corner of the professor's smoked turkey and Brie sandwich.

From there they moved on to Washington Square. The little park was appallingly crowded. There were young people tossing frisbees by the fountain and old people on benches holding their faces to the sun. There were steel drummers, Italian-ice vendors, hot-dog vendors, skateboarders, Rollerbladers, NYU students on break from studying for finals, artists doing cheap portraits of tourists, jugglers, folk singers, pantomimes, countless dog walkers—and, waiting by the chess tables in the southwest corner, Rodney and his professor.

The very first thing out of Rodney's mouth was:

"It never gets this bad uptown."

"This is highly unusual," Gulliver said stiffly. "On weekdays it's very civilized."

Things only went downhill from there. As soon as one of the chess tables opened up, Professor Moroni suggested putting the dogs in the nearby fenced-in dog run.

"More fun for them than having to sit," he said.

Never in his life had Gulliver been stuck in the dog run. On some days it might have been tolerable, but this afternoon it was full of mutts—a fact Rodney didn't fail to point out. "We have very few mutts uptown," he murmured.

If this wasn't aggravating enough, the first non-mutt they encountered was a female greyhound with about as much conversation as a squirrel. Then came a female Pekingese who giggled idiotically at whatever they said. Then a basset hound who drooled while bragging about a kennel club show he'd seen on TV.

"We don't have a TV in the apartment," Rodney murmured when they got rid of the basset.

"Neither do we!" Gulliver almost shouted.

Gulliver fought the impulse, but eventually he couldn't resist asking if Rodney spoke German. Rodney nodded his well-shaped head—though of course he didn't really speak the language. He'd made up *Gotten Grog* on the spur of the moment, the German sound of it having sprung magically from the distant German roots of the schnauzer breed.

"French?" Gulliver asked uneasily.

"Gourmet," said Rodney.

"Excuse me?"

"'Gourmet' is a French word."

"Is that all you know?"

In fact, it was. Rodney looked away, as if distracted by a squirrel racing around a tree trunk.

"*Quel dommage,*" Gulliver murmured.

From the sound of it, Rodney figured this meant "What a pity." He murmured back:

"*Kurten Zog.*"

Poor Gulliver. Now he was at a total loss.

"Look at those fools," Rodney said, pointing his snout at a gaggle of people admiring the work of one of the sidewalk portrait painters. "They think *that's* art. They should see our collection."

Gulliver didn't take the bait and ask about it, but this didn't stop Rodney.

"It's pretty spectacular. Mostly modern. Though, to tell you the truth, my personal favorite's this old print in the bathroom. *Riding to the Hounds*, it's called. It has three people in it, three horses, and twenty-seven dogs."

Gulliver couldn't top this. But just as he was about

to throw in the towel on
the conversation, a
faint rumble drew
his eyes skyward.
High overhead
a jet plane was
leaving behind a
trail of exhaust as
white and fluffy as . . .

"Chloe," he murmured.

"Excuse me?" said
Rodney.

"Oh, I was just day-
dreaming about Chloe.
Do you fly much?"

"Fly? I'm a dog, not a duck!"

"I mean in jets."

"Oh. Well, one time we flew to a place called Maine.
We rented a house there. Ocean view."

Gulliver rose to his full height. "We fly to Paris every
July."

"Paris?"

"France."

"Really?"

"We swap apartments with a French professor every
July."

At this, Rodney's impressive mustache finally

drooped a bit. You couldn't live with an art history professor without knowing what Paris was.

Gulliver was suddenly perking up. But just as he started to gloat, up shot the schnauzer's snout again.

"How long's the flight?"

"About seven hours going, over eight coming back."

"Poor you."

"Poor me?"

"Stuck in a carrying case all that time. It must be hellish."

What was hellish was having this schnauzer pity him for getting to fly off to Paris every summer! Never had Gulliver been so irritated.

"You wouldn't say that if you knew Chloe," he said. "Maltese. Eyes black as raisins. Cutest little nose you've ever seen. Lives with Madame Courgette, owner of Le Petit Café."

Rodney found Malteses adorable, so this shut him up for a minute. Nor did his mood improve when he looked through the chicken-wire fence at the chess tables. His professor was playing the white pieces, and Gulliver's professor had captured more white than his had black.

"Mine's a little rusty," Rodney said when Professor Moroni's king was toppled. "He hasn't played in ages."

"Neither has mine," Gulliver said. "But he's rustproof."

Gulliver had to eat a bit of crow when Professor Moroni won the next game. But Professor Rattigan won the third, and then the fourth, too.

After this the professors yielded the table to a pair of waiting players and collected the dogs.

"Would you have time for a cup of tea?" Professor Rattigan asked.

"That would be nice," said Professor Moroni.

On their way across the square a glorious thing happened. A man in a saffron robe caught sight of Gulliver and bowed low, holding his hands together in prayer. This had happened a few times before, but in front of Rodney it was particularly gratifying.

"What in the name of dog was that about?" Rodney asked.

Gulliver couldn't help smiling at this expression, which he'd never heard before. "We're considered sacred," he said.

Rodney's eyes widened in spite of himself.

"In Tibet it's believed that when our human companion dies," Gulliver said, "his soul enters our body."

"It can get in through all that hair?"

Gulliver rose above this remark.

"Hey, Dr. Rattigan," Carlos said, opening the brass door of One Fifth Avenue for them. "Hey, Gully, see you've got a friend."

"Gully?" Rodney murmured, smirking.

"He doesn't know any better," Gulliver said as they crossed the cool lobby. "He's only a doorman."

Rodney let this drop, for the doorman at his building had been known to call him Rod. But when they got out of the elevator he said, "What floor is this?"

"Seventeen."

"That's all?"

"What do you mean?" Gulliver said.

"We're on forty-eight. The penthouse."

And as soon as they stepped into the living room, Rodney looked around and said, "My goodness, how old-fashioned."

"Everything you see is a valuable antique," Gulliver snapped.

"Really. We believe in 'Out with the old, in with the new.'"

Professor Rattigan went into the kitchen to make tea, giving Professor Moroni a chance to look over the library.

"Nearly all first editions," Gulliver told Rodney in an undertone.

"But where are your art books?" Rodney asked.

"We like literature."

From the books, Professor Moroni moved on to four small oil paintings hanging over the mantelpiece. Rodney commented that they were awfully conservative.

"You think so?" Gulliver said. "Two are by genuine Old Masters."

"Which ones?" Rodney asked sharply.

To be honest, Gulliver had no idea. But he knew that if you sound definite, dogs generally believe you.

"The landscape and the still life."

"Hmph," Rodney said. "How many rooms do you have here, anyway?"

"Five, not counting the kitchen and the foyer. What about you?"

"We have six."

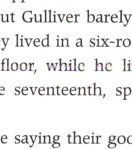

Along with the tea Professor Rattigan brought out a plate of cookies and a Genoa salami, and both professors slipped their dogs a slice of the salami. But Gulliver barely touched his. The thought that Rodney lived in a six-room penthouse on the forty-eighth floor, while he lived in a five-room apartment on the seventeenth, spoiled his appetite.

When the professors were saying their goodbyes at the door, Professor Moroni suggested a rematch.

"Never have to wait for a table at my place," he said. "Though I'm afraid home-field advantage won't help much against you. Shall we say next Saturday at three?"

"Perfect," Professor Rattigan said.

"Bring your dog. They seem to get on well together."

Of course the dogs didn't pick up any of this. In fact, Gulliver was bidding Rodney farewell in the fervent hope that he would never have to lay eyes on the irksome schnauzer again.

The
Forty-eighth Floor

If you'd asked him, Gulliver would have said his favorite sounds were operatic, but in truth his favorite sounds were the whirr of the electric can opener, which meant Prime Premium, and the jangle of his leash being taken down from its peg, which meant a walk. Just as he never overate, however—never gobbled his food as ill-bred dogs did—he didn't like to overwalk. Once around Washington Square suited him perfectly. His legs were not long.

But the weather that next Saturday afternoon was so pleasant that Professor Rattigan decided it would be healthy to walk uptown to Professor Moroni's. Off they headed up Fifth Avenue. By Twenty-third Street, Gulliver's back legs were already tired. Block after block they walked till finally, at Thirty-fourth Street, Gulliver put his paw down, refusing to step off the curb onto the crosswalk.

"Okay, okay," Professor Rattigan said, lifting an arm to hail a cab.

The cab was nicely air-conditioned, and at the end of the ride the cabbie pulled up right next to the curb, so Gulliver didn't have to execute an undignified leap over the gutter. He'd thought perhaps they were heading for the public library, but there was no wide staircase flanked by stone lions. Instead, they were in front of a sleek, glossy building that stretched up ominously into the sky.

Having a sudden sickening feeling that it was Rodney's building, Gulliver again refused to budge.

"What's the matter with you today?" Professor Rattigan said, giving the leash a good tug as a young, pimply doorman opened a tinted-glass door for them.

The doorman put through a call and pointed them to an elevator that was all chrome-and-mirrors instead of wood paneling. It shot up so fast it made Gulliver's stomach queasy. And he only felt queasier when the doors opened and there, in the doorway to a penthouse apartment, stood Rodney and his professor. The only plus was that Rodney looked rather queasy himself.

The truth was, Rodney had never dreamed his professor would actually invite this other professor and his dog over.

The penthouse was bright and colorful, with sunlight pouring through plate-glass windows onto shiny floors, onto chairs made of gleaming fiberglass and molded plywood, onto works of art Gulliver had never seen the like of. One painting was striped like a rainbow and shaped like a dog biscuit! Even the chess pieces—a board was set out on a plexiglass table—were dazzling: magenta and lemon yellow instead of black and white. And yet the apartment wasn't half the square footage of their place at One Fifth Avenue. Rodney had been telling the truth about the print in the bathroom—it did have twenty-seven dogs in it—but he'd been fudging when he'd said there were six rooms besides the kitchen and foyer. There were only four, and they weren't all that spacious.

"I thought you included closets," Rodney muttered.

Gulliver smiled under his mustache. "Those books are certainly big," he said, inclining his head toward a bookshelf.

"Those are his art books," Rodney said.

"He doesn't have any regular books?"

Rodney scowled.

"The color scheme certainly is . . . loud," Gulliver said.

"We hate stodgy. Come see the view."

Rodney led the way to the spare bedroom—Professor Moroni's daughter stayed there when she visited—and hopped up onto a bed under a window. The view from there was spectacular, but Gulliver couldn't help thinking it was a bit unnatural. The buses and taxis on the avenue below looked like chew toys. In fact, it struck him that there was something a bit vulgar about being up so high. Whereas the seventeenth floor seemed in perfect taste: high enough to be above the hustle and bustle, yet not so high that you couldn't tell a Saint Bernard from a beagle.

When they got back to the living room, the professors were hunched over the chessboard.

"How was your week?" Gulliver asked graciously.

"Well," Rodney said, "I talked to a very pretty toy poodle on my walk yesterday. You?"

"I had a long conversation with a lovely Norfolk terrier on Tuesday." In fact, she'd had a scruffy coat, but there was no reason to pass this on to Rodney. "Have your summer plans solidified?"

"I think we're staying here," Rodney muttered. "I'm not sure."

Gulliver waited for him to ask about his, but Rodney just stared darkly at the chess players. After a minute Professor Rattigan clucked his tongue and said, "Sorry, old man. Checkmate."

Professor Moroni groaned as his king fell. Rodney winced.

"We take off for Paris in a few weeks," Gulliver murmured.

Le Petit Café

Rodney made a good point about the misery of being stuck in a carrying case for a whole transatlantic flight. For some reason, airlines frown on dogs traveling in the cabins of planes, so they stow them in a pressurized hold down below, separated from everything and everyone familiar. On his first trip, when he was just a few months old, Gulliver spent the whole flight shivering in terror. Fortunately, Professor Rattigan noticed his condition at the airport in Paris, and for the flight back, and every subsequent flight, he'd given Gulliver a tranquilizer.

They always took the overnight flight, and this year, as usual, Gulliver didn't come out of his sleepy haze till they were in a cab heading for their Parisian apartment. It was in a lovely neighborhood called Saint-Germain, where the average building was far shorter than the average building in Manhattan. So instead of living on the seventeenth floor, they lived on the fifth. And instead of a doorman, the building was watched over by a little gray-haired woman called a "concierge." And instead of a wood-paneled elevator, they rode up in a sort of bronze birdcage.

Though smaller than theirs, the French professor's apartment had its charms, notably the living-room sofa. It was upholstered in horsehair, which was miraculously warm on cool days and miraculously cool on hot days. After their morning walk in the nearby Luxembourg Gardens, Professor Rattigan would retire to the study to work on his novel and Gulliver would settle on the horsehair sofa. It had an excellent view of a wall covered by a medieval tapestry that featured a queenly figure with two elegant whippets at her feet.

But it was the evenings, not the days, that made Paris special. In July, Paris can be steamy, but although the sun stays up till after ten o'clock, things usually begin to cool off around eight. This was when they headed back out. They walked over to the river and turned west, passing bright yellow postboxes and bright red-and-white fire hydrants. Soon the blue-and-white-striped awning of Le Petit Café came into view—and both of their hearts beat faster.

It would be hard to say which of them enjoyed their evenings at the café more. Professor Rattigan had the company of the beautiful Madeline de Crecy, who taught

English literature at a nearby university called the Sorbonne. Professor de Crecy was allergic to long-haired dogs, so even if Gulliver had wanted to sit obediently under their table, he wouldn't have been allowed to. But why would he want to do that when he could flirt with a stunning Maltese over by the door to the kitchen?

Few things in life are sweeter than being able to impress the dog you love. The only places Chloe had ever been to were Paris and the sleepy French seaside village where Madame Courgette spent August, when the restaurant was closed. Gulliver, too, divided his time between only two places. But *his* two places were Paris and New York. How could Chloe compete? She could tell him about the fishing nets pulled up on the beach and the joys of splashing in the backwash and chasing seagulls. But he had the greatest city in the world at his bark and call.

Just across from the restaurant an ancient stone bridge spanned the river Seine. It could hardly have been more picturesque, but compared to the soaring bridges of New York City—the Brooklyn Bridge, for instance, or the George Washington Bridge—it was a toy. To the west of the restaurant the Eiffel Tower loomed up. But impressive as it was, it was barely half as tall as the Empire State Building. Gulliver had never splashed in the sea or chased a gull, but he'd seen the Statue of Liberty and the United Nations, and he lived right on Fifth Avenue. And though Cheveux de Chien, the Parisian groomer his professor took him to once every July, was perfectly nice, it wasn't half as up-to-date as Groom-o-rama.

Madame Courgette treated him like a prince. He and his professor came to the café almost every night during July, and his professor always ordered many courses and expensive bottles of wine and left American-sized tips. So at least once every evening Madame Courgette would slip Gulliver some delicacy, a perfectly cooked medallion of pork, or a nicely sautéed piece of veal.

In fact, life in Paris was so pleasant that Gulliver always hated to see the month come to an end.

"I wish you would come over to visit," he would tell Chloe.

"*Moi aussi,*" Chloe would say. "Me, too."

This year his last evening at Le Petit Café was more sentimental than usual. He wasn't as young a dog as he used to be; he really would have liked to make his relationship with Chloe more permanent. And Chloe looked particularly fetching with two pale pink ribbons in her hair. So he told her he wished Madame Courgette would open a restaurant in New York. "It would do great business, I'm sure. New Yorkers love French cuisine."

Chloe reminded him that Madame Courgette spoke no English. Then she let out a lovely sigh and said she couldn't believe they wouldn't see each other for almost seven (dog) years.

It was all very distressful. But at the same time highly enjoyable.

By coincidence, Professor Rattigan was experiencing feelings very similar to Gulliver's. Every year, as July wound down, he would try to convince Professor de Crecy to move to New York. Her English was perfect: New York University would be lucky to get her. But she always said she was happy with her job in Paris.

This year, after their dessert dishes were cleared away, Professor Rattigan laid his hand over hers. Like Gulliver, he wasn't as young as he used to be. In fact, he'd recently had to yank some gray hairs out of his blond beard.

He took a healthy swig of his cognac. "Tell me, Madeline," he said, "would you consider coming to New York as my wife?"

Home Sweet Home

There was nothing unusual in the fact that Professor Rattigan talked to Gulliver while packing his bags later that night. But normally he talked in a lighthearted way, chuckling at his own little jokes. Tonight his tone was as soft and soothing as the one a veterinarian uses just before sticking you with a needle.

Gulliver decided his professor must be trying to treat him with kid gloves after his sad parting scene with Chloe.

The next morning Professor Rattigan ground up a tranquilizer in Gulliver's breakfast, and by the time Gulliver was in his carrying case, he was already woozy. When he came around, the carrying case was jouncing on the backseat of a cab. The radio was blaring a traffic report (". . . bumper-to-bumper on the Kosciusko Bridge"), and the smell of the air was pure New York City.

Awful as saying goodbye to Chloe was, there was something comforting about getting out of the cab in front of One Fifth Avenue. Usually it was hot and humid when they returned from Europe, but that evening was very pleasant.

"Welcome back, Dr. Rattigan," said Carlos the doorman. "That you in there, Gully?"

Though Gulliver would never have admitted it to Rodney, or Chloe for that matter, there was something a little degrading about being lugged around in a carrying case. It was like a mini–jail cell announcing to the world that the prisoner can't be trusted to behave on the outside. So it was a relief when Professor Rattigan set the case down right there in the lobby and opened the door.

Most dogs would have bolted out. But bolting, in Gulliver's opinion, was undignified, so he stretched a couple of times and ambled out nonchalantly, as if he'd only wandered in by chance a moment earlier. He was glad of this when he saw the elderly female cocker spaniel who lived in the other seventeenth-floor apartment eyeing him from the doorway to the mail room. She was one of the most civilized dogs in the building.

The professor and the doorman were having a conversation, so Gulliver wandered over her way. Her leash holder, a plump woman named Ms. Tavendish who was always making googly eyes at his professor, was chattering away with the building's superintendent.

"Been away?" the cocker spaniel asked.

"Paris," Gulliver said, suppressing a yawn.

"Fun?"

"Marvelous. How was July here?"

"Hot. It only cooled down yesterday. But we got out to the Hamptons a couple of times."

Gulliver stretched. "Just had an eight-hour flight," he explained.

"My goodness. Jet lag?"

"Not really. I took a pill."

"See a lot of French poodles over there?"

They talked quite a while, for Ms. Tavendish had a lot to say to the super, and Professor Rattigan seemed to have an unusual amount to say to the doorman. But at last the professor clucked his tongue and picked up the carrying case. Though the birdcage elevator in Paris was quaintly charming, it was slow and jerky. It was good to be back in one that ran smoothly. Good to be back in their own apartment, too. It was a little hot and stuffy at first, but Professor Rattigan turned on the air-conditioning before taking him on a much-needed walk, and by the time they returned, the place was comfortably cool.

It was also a comfort to have some Prime Premium, which was unavailable in France. The scraps he got at the café were exotic but often so rich they played tricks on his digestion.

The professor ordered in Thai food for his own dinner and then, after taking Gulliver out again, settled down to read his mail. He got through less than half of it. He was still on Paris time, six hours later, and soon went yawning off to bed.

Gulliver followed suit. But heavenly as it was to be curled up in his own bed, he wasn't all that sleepy after dozing the entire day. Eventually he padded off to the kitchen for a midnight snack. Then he hopped up onto a chair under one of the windows in the living room, rested his paws on the sill, and gazed out to the east. The city's glow blotted out all except a handful of stars. But Paris, he knew, had the same problem. Was Chloe looking at those same few stars, so upset about his departure that she had insomnia?

He sighed happily at the thought. She really was the most beautiful dog imaginable. How she'd laughed at his joke about Labradoodles! And that was a good one she'd told him about parking meters being pay toilets—he would have to pass it on to Rodney. He leaned his head close to the window and peered northward. Was that glowing skyscraper up there Rodney's building? He hoped their professors would arrange a chess game soon so he could tell Rodney all about his trip. Had they been up to Maine? If so, he supposed he would have to hear about Rodney's trip. But then Maine could hardly compare to Paris.

A yawn escaped him. He padded back into the bedroom and curled up in his bed. "Night, Chloe," he murmured under his breath.

He yawned again but still didn't fall straight to sleep.
It was too much fun luxuriating in the delicious pain of
being separated from his beloved.

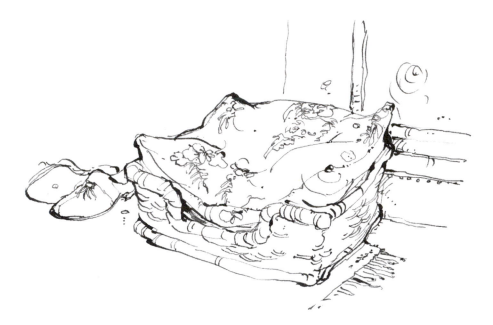

Queens

The next day even started out strangely. Professor Rattigan, still being on Paris time, rose very early, and Gulliver, who'd stayed up so late, slept in. By the time he woke up, he was alone in the apartment.

Of course there was fresh Prime Premium in his bowl. And though he would have liked a walk, it wasn't crucial. The professor wouldn't start teaching again for over a month, so Gulliver was quite sure he would be home soon. He made a slow tour of the apartment, reacquainting himself with all its lovely nooks and hiding places, then curled up in a wing chair.

His professor got home at one o'clock. But instead of taking him for his walk, he did a most peculiar thing. He brought Gulliver's bed out of the bedroom and carried it out of the apartment. A few minutes later he returned, and this time he took away the carrying case! A few minutes after this, he came back and pulled Gulliver's leash off its peg.

"Let's go for a last walk, boy," he said.

Gulliver cocked his head to one side, wondering why his professor sounded so somber.

The substitute doorman was on duty downstairs, an old man with a face as wrinkly as a Chinese shar-pei's. He said hello to Professor Rattigan but neglected to greet Gulliver, barely glancing down at him, so Gulliver resolved to snub the old coot on his way back in.

Sadly, he never got the chance. After they'd done their tour of Washington Square Park, Professor Rattigan led him to a black town car with tinted windows parked on Waverly Place. A driver in a cap hopped out and opened one of the back doors for them.

So that was it, Gulliver thought, sitting up alertly on the backseat as they drove away. His professor missed his French lady friend as much as he missed his Chloe, so they were flying back to Paris. And for a longer stay than before, since they were evidently taking his bed as well as his carrying case. Could they be

40

moving there permanently? That would be a shock. After all, New York City—not Paris—was the center of the
modern world. On the other hand, he would be able to
see Chloe regularly. . . .

By the time they were in the Midtown Tunnel,
Gulliver had made peace with this sudden upheaval in
his life. Knowing his professor, he was sure they would
be coming back to One Fifth Avenue for visits. His only
real regret was not being able to tell Rodney about the
move. It would have been fun to say, "Oh, I'll be in Europe for a while . . ."

It was hard to see much through the tinted windows,
but he was pretty sure they were on the same highway
they'd taken in from JFK airport yesterday. However,
when the car finally stopped and the driver hopped out
and opened the door for them, there wasn't an airline
terminal in sight. They were on a block where shabby,
two-story houses peered glumly at each other across a
street with more than its share of potholes. Not at all the
sort of neighborhood they would normally have visited.

Yet Professor Rattigan got out of the car. "Come on,
boy," he said, giving Gulliver's leash a tug.

Gulliver descended dubiously onto a curb separated
from a sidewalk by a strip of patchy grass that clearly
hadn't been watered all month. They proceeded down a
cracked, uneven sidewalk till the professor said, "426A,
guess this is it."

The house before them had a door on street level and another up a flight of rickety-looking stairs. It was sided in hideous, lime-green asphalt shingles, and the mustard-colored paint on the street-level door was peeling. The professor knocked on it.

No one answered. The professor pushed a buzzer.

"Bring it around back, will you?" shouted an oddly familiar voice.

Between this shabby house and the one next door was a passageway choked with dried-out weeds. As they proceeded down it, the noise level grew. Kids screeched, dogs barked, and a sportscaster cried, "It's long, it's high, it's . . . outta here!"

"Sounds lively, doesn't it, boy?" the professor said.

They stopped at a chain-link gate to a backyard as active as Washington Square on a sunny Sunday. Splashing in one of those plastic, aboveground pools were four or five human children with skin colors ranging from the pink of Chloe's ribbons to the brown of Beef and Liver Delight. Parked in lawn chairs around a picnic table with a boom box blaring a baseball game was a similar assortment of adults. They were all drinking beer—the men out of bottles, the women out of glasses—except for an ancient black woman who sat calmly stroking a calico cat in her lap. Barking and running in circles around the pool were three huge, mangy-looking mutts.

The biggest dog of all bounded over to the gate and

growled at a shocked Gulliver. A man turned down the volume on the ball game and jumped out of his lawn chair.

"Dr. Rattigan! I'm so sorry! I thought you were the pizza guy!"

Gulliver didn't immediately recognize their doorman. He associated him with the lobby of One Fifth Avenue, and instead of a charcoal-gray uniform with burgundy piping the man had on shorts, flip-flops, and a loud, half-unbuttoned Hawaiian shirt.

"Shut up, Frankie," Carlos said, grabbing the big mutt by the collar. He opened the gate. "We're having a little birthday party. Juanita's eight today. Nita, come say hi to Dr. Rattigan."

A brown-skinned girl clambered out of the pool and raced toward them, crying, "Is that Gully?"

Just inside the gate was a bush with dusty leaves and, beyond that, a motorbike draped with a tarp. But before Gulliver could take refuge behind either one, the dripping-wet girl had him in her arms.

"You're so cute!" she cried, nearly squeezing the life out of him. "This is the best birthday present in the world!"

As Gulliver squirmed to escape, another child clambered out of the pool, a brown-skinned boy slightly larger than his torturer.

"He's not just yours!" the boy cried, yanking Gulliver out of her arms.

"Pedro's right, he's everybody's," the doorman said. "Just like Frankie and Pudge and Pogo."

"And guess who'll end up feeding and brushing him," said a woman wearing a sun hat.

"Dr. Rattigan, I'd like you to meet my wife, Consuela," said the doorman.

"Please, Dr. Rattigan, sit and have a beer," Consuela said, shaking the professor's hand.

Professor Rattigan was a wine drinker, not a beer drinker, but it seemed only polite to accept the invitation, since they were doing him such a favor. When he'd arrived back at One Fifth Avenue yesterday, he'd stopped to talk to the doorman and told him he was soon to be engaged.

"Gosh, Dr. Rattigan," Carlos had said, "I always figured you were too smart to fall into the same trap as the rest of us."

"Well, I think you'll understand when you see the lady," Professor Rattigan had said, smiling.

"When's she coming?"

"Next week, just for a visit. Then we're going to France to visit her family, then back here in early September. But the reason I bring it up is, there's a hitch. She's allergic to long-haired dogs. I thought maybe you could spread the word among the tenants, see if anyone might want to adopt that gorgeous fellow over there." He'd pointed at Gulliver, who'd been over by the mail room with his neighbor's cocker spaniel.

"I'll spread the word, sir. But if nobody steps up to the plate, we'd take him."

"You? Really?"

"Sure."

"Where do you live, Carlos?"

"Astoria, out in Queens. We've got three dogs already, but the more the merrier. I always liked Gully. Can't believe you'd give him up."

"It breaks my heart, believe me. In a lot of ways he's my closest friend. But I don't really have any choice."

"Guess not. So you want me to spread the word?"

"Not if you're serious about your offer."

"He's had his shots and all that stuff?"

"Of course."

On seeing the neighborhood and the house, Professor Rattigan had had qualms about leaving his beloved pet here, but the cheerful atmosphere in the backyard reassured him. There seemed to be three families at the party: the Montoyas—Carlos and his wife and two kids; and a very dark couple from the West Indies named Ponson who lived on the top floor with their son and the elderly woman, evidently a grandmother; and a Polish-American family from across the street named Sewinski. They were all very friendly, and though Gulliver seemed a bit dismayed at being fought over by wet children, the professor suspected he would soon be lapping up all the attention. In fact, he felt a pang to think how soon the dog would forget all about him and his former dull existence.

"I owe you for this, Carlos," he said. "You'll have to think of some way for me to repay you."

"Oh, it's no problem," Carlos said. But after a moment he added, "Well, actually . . ."

"Yes?"

"You wouldn't know anybody at the Columbia School of Journalism, would you?"

"I know the head of the program."

"Wow. The thing is, I always wanted to be a journalist — write for newspapers, you know."

"I suppose it's never too late. Though I suspect most of the student body would be quite a bit younger than you."

"Oh, jeez, not me! I'm not stupid, I know it's too late for me. I'm talking about my oldest kid. *Roberto!*"

In a moment a door opened to what looked like a toolshed in the rear of the backyard. Out came a boy, or rather a young man, wearing cargo shorts and a Planet Hollywood T-shirt. He had a shaved head and a silver earring in one ear.

"Roberto, meet Dr. Rattigan," Carlos said. "He's a professor at NYU, and he knows the head of the Columbia School of Journalism."

Roberto seemed less thrilled about the connection

than his father did, but he shook the professor's hand politely and told him about the classes he'd taken last term at Queens College.

"When are you going to give the kids your surprise, Robbie?" Consuela asked quietly.

"Now, if you want," Roberto said. "Good to meet you, Dr. Rattigan." He pointed at Gulliver, trapped in Pedro's arms. "Cool dog."

When Roberto disappeared back into his hut, the ancient black woman grinned, showing yellow snaggleteeth.

"Roberto going to be fine journalist," she said in a singsong voice. "You will see."

"Granny's always right, you know," said Mr. Ponson.

When Carlos explained that Roberto was living at home to save money for journalism school, Professor Rattigan said, "Speaking of money, I'm going to send you a regular check to pay for Gulliver's Prime Premium."

Consuela hooted. "You think Frankie and Pudge would let him get a bite of that? But don't you worry, we'll take good care of the sweet little guy."

Pedro had finally set the sweet little guy down. Wet, bedraggled, and stunned,

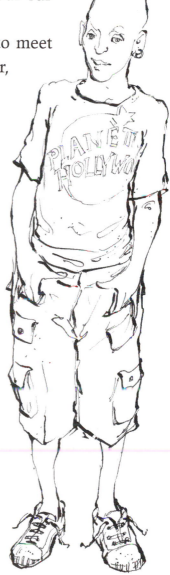

Gulliver was quickly surrounded by the three towering mutts, all of whom sniffed at him in the crudest possible manner. The two largest, Frankie and Pudge, looked as if they were part Lab, part rottweiler. The other, slightly smaller but still twice his size, looked as if she was a mix of about six different breeds.

"What's your name?" she asked.

"Gulliver," Gulliver said.

Pudge and Frankie snorted, but the female said, "I'm Pogo. You like salsa?"

"Who's Salsa?"

"The music," she said.

Thanks to the lowered volume on the baseball game, music could be heard blaring from another backyard. Gulliver frowned at the thumping beat.

"We prefer classical."

"What's that?" Frankie growled.

"Is it like reggae?" Pogo said. "I love reggae."

Gulliver, who'd never heard of reggae, made a snap decision not to waste his breath on these undereducated mongrels. He just smiled vaguely beneath his mustache and shot a look at his professor, wondering how much longer they were going to have to suffer this barbaric atmosphere.

Catching Gulliver's look, Professor Rattigan experienced a peculiar sensation. Here he was, a distinguished professor, soon to be married to the woman of his dreams, and suddenly he was on the verge of bursting into tears in front of his doorman. He took a swig of beer and rose to his feet.

"I think I'll be going, if you don't mind," he said. "I don't really care for long goodbyes."

"Pizza's coming," Consuela said temptingly.

But Professor Rattigan wasn't a pizza eater.

"I know how you must feel about your dog, sir," Carlos said sympathetically, standing up with him.

Professor Rattigan would have liked to make light of the situation. He would have liked to pick Gulliver up and say with a smile, "Don't hold it against me, old boy. Remember—to err is human, to forgive canine." But he couldn't do it. If he picked Gulliver up, he knew he would turn into a blubbering mess. So he simply told Mrs. Montoya and the others that it had been a pleasure to meet them and wished Juanita a happy birthday.

If Juanita heard him, she didn't acknowledge it. She and Pedro were now on a small trampoline behind the pool, screeching with glee as they bounced each other higher and higher into the air.

"I brought his carrying case and bed," Professor Rattigan said.

"Come through this way," said Carlos.

As Professor Rattigan followed his doorman into the house, he couldn't help casting one last look over his shoulder. But what with Gulliver surrounded by his new canine friends, all he saw of him was his stubby, happily wagging tail.

"How soon they forget," Professor Rattigan thought wistfully.

First Faint

Gulliver's tail *was* moving, but it wasn't wagging happily, it was quivering anxiously. When he'd been encircled by larger dogs in the past, they'd always been on leashes. These smelly mutts had no human beings to restrain them. If they took it into their empty heads, they could rip him to pieces.

"Where'd you get the fancy-schmancy collar?" Pudge asked.

Little as Gulliver felt like conversing, it was impossible to ignore such a direct question. "He brought it back for me from a trip," he murmured.

"Who?" said Pogo.

"Him," Gulliver said, stepping back for a view of his professor.

But no professor was in sight, which made the long hair on the back of his neck stand straight up. Only for a second, however. Their doorman wasn't around either. He must have taken the professor into the house to show him something. Or to conduct some sort of business. That probably explained this bizarre stopover on the way to the airport.

"Where do you live?" Pogo asked.

"New York City," Gulliver said. "And Paris."

"This is New York City."

"I mean Manhattan, of course."

"Queens is as much New York City as Manhattan," Frankie declared.

"Whatever you say," Gulliver murmured, not about to argue such a point. "Excuse me, will you?"

There was a gap between Pudge and Pogo, and he slipped through it. As he approached the old woman, the cat in her lap hissed at him.

Gulliver stationed himself right by the gate, hoping the professor would get the hint when he came back out. Soon another child climbed out of the pool and headed for him, a nasty-looking pink-skinned boy with a missing tooth and white cream on his nose.

"He's mine!" Juanita shouted.

She raced over from the trampoline, and the two kids almost pulled poor Gulliver limb from limb.

"Chris, it's Juanita's birthday," Mr. Sewinski said sharply, and the nasty-looking boy, scowling, released Gulliver's hindquarters.

"Such a sweet doggie," Juanita said, carrying him back to the trampoline.

To Gulliver's immense relief, he was set down again. Unfortunately, he didn't seem to be on quite firm ground. A slick material wobbled under his paws.

Juanita and her brother, Pedro, began jumping up and down on either side of him. He shot into the air. When he came down, it was all he could do to land on his paws. The devilish children screamed with delight,

and before he knew it, he was in the air again. This time he lost his bearings entirely and landed—*ooomph!*—on his left side. Up he went again, now totally disoriented. The instant before he touched down for a third time, both kids landed, turning the ground into a springboard that instantly sent him back up and sideways, up, up . . .

When he hit the pool, the concussion dazed him. He gasped—and got a mouthful of water.

Hands clenched his chest. He was hoisted into the air by the nasty boy with the missing tooth.

"Don't kill the poor thing his first day," Consuela advised.

Juanita yanked Gulliver away from the boy. "That cool you off, Gully?" she said.

Shocked out of his wits, Gulliver was suddenly on the ground again. This time it felt solid.

"Look at him!" said Frankie the mutt.

"He looks more like a rat than a dog!"

Gulliver shook himself violently, spraying water in all directions. He'd caught sight of himself in the mirror at Groom-o-rama

after his scented bath and knew that the
foul mutt wasn't far off the mark. When his
splendid coat was matted down and stuck
to his body, he looked pathetically small
and skinny.

It was simply too much to bear.
Utterly desperate, he resorted to
unheard-of behavior. He let out a bark.

It wasn't impressive. In fact, some might have called
it more of a yap than a bark. But it came from the depths
of his beleaguered heart.

Yet not even this brought his professor back. Gulliver
stared through a screen door into the ground-floor
apartment. No one was visible inside. Had the professor
gone up to the top floor?

"Look, he wants to scope out our place," said Mr.
Ponson, laughing as Gulliver headed up a set of outdoor stairs.

"He fit through okay," old Mrs. Ponson predicted.

The elderly woman was right. Gulliver managed to
squeeze through the cat-sized pet flap in the door at the
top of the stairs. He found himself in an unpleasantly
hot kitchen with a funny smell, rotting and spicy at the
same time. He moved on to the Ponsons' cramped living room. Then three small bedrooms. The whole place
had the kind of furniture people left out on Manhattan
sidewalks for garbage pickup. At One Fifth Avenue they

had two bathrooms for one person; here there was one bathroom for four. There was hardly a book to be seen, and no Old Masters on the walls, just a bunch of framed family photos, none of any interest except for one, hung between the living-room windows, that showed a grinning black man standing in front of a shop with the Eiffel Tower looming in the background. It was a comfort to see something familiar. But Gulliver didn't linger, still certain he would soon be seeing the real thing.

Up to this point cats had played little part in his life. He'd heard a few alley cats howling at night in Paris, and during a youthful visit to the veterinarian for shots he'd seen a just-declawed cat with bandaged front paws. But when he got back to the kitchen, the calico cat was stationed in front of the pet flap—and she definitely had not been declawed. In fact, she looked quite vicious.

Though he didn't know it, Gulliver was facing a defining moment. If he cowered now, the cat would have his number forever. But just then all he cared about was finding his professor, so he walked up to the beast without so much as flinching. And small as he was compared to the mutts, he was at least bigger than this cat.

She hissed, but moved aside to let him pass.

At the foot of the stairs Gulliver made straight for the first-floor back door. It had a much bigger pet flap than upstairs, but the kitchen beyond it was just as hot as the one above. Hadn't anyone in Queens heard about air-conditioning? Gulliver walked into a living room that featured a tattered sofa, a La-Z-Boy recliner, and a gigantic TV set. Then he checked three dumpy, depressing bedrooms. In Pedro's a pair of goldfish swam around in a bowl, and in Juanita's a tiny furry creature in a cage on the desk squeaked in dismay at the sight of him. But they were the only living creatures in evidence.

As Gulliver was passing back through the living room, the click of the front door gave him a jolt of hope. But when the door opened, it revealed not his professor but the doorman—with Gulliver's carrying case under one arm and his bed under the other! What in the name of dog were they doing here instead of on their way, with him, to Paris?

The doorman came in and closed the door with his foot, preventing Gulliver from dashing out.

"You could get run over out on the street, boy."

Gulliver fled back through the kitchen and out the screen flap.

"Look at him go!" Consuela said, laughing as Gulliver dashed across the backyard.

The mutts laughed, too, but Gulliver hardly heard. There was only one place left where the professor might be: the toolshed that had produced the college kid. Gulliver sprinted between the pool and the trampoline and hurled himself in the open door.

The toolshed was a bedroom, the walls plastered with movie posters. The boy was inspecting himself in a dresser mirror.

"Hey," he said, turning.

It wasn't the boy. It was a monster with bright red woolly hair, a huge round red nose, a white mouth bigger than a banana, and feet the size of dachshunds.

Gulliver passed out.

Faint #2

Carlos and Consuela figured Roberto was saving up quite a bit of money for journalism school, since over the summer he was working five nights a week in the ticket booth at the Forest Hills Multiplex. They were wrong. He actually worked only four nights a week, and half of what he made went for the acting class he took when he snuck into Manhattan on Thursdays. The truth was, Roberto didn't want to be a journalist any more than he wanted to spend his life selling tickets to the movies. He wanted to be *in* the movies. What money he managed to put away was for his move to Hollywood.

His acting teacher, Ms. Treadle, encouraged her students to use every opportunity to sharpen their skills. So on that sunny Sunday he was about to entertain his little sister and the other kids with a clown act. But when he saw the dog faint, he took off his wig and fake nose.

"Did I scare you?" he said, picking up the limp animal. Roberto sat on the bed and stroked its damp fur. "See, just me," he said when Gulliver opened his eyes.

Wriggling in the strange lap, Gulliver craned his head. There was a small bathroom in a corner of the hut, but the door was open, and the professor wasn't inside.

"Escaping 'the madding crowd's ignoble strife,'" said Roberto, who often read poetry aloud to improve his diction. "You can hide out here if you want while I do my act. Just don't take a leak on the bed, okay?"

Setting the dog aside, Roberto put his wig and clown nose back on and left. Gulliver remained behind, trembling on the sheet. The logical explanation for this nightmare situation was that these awful people had taken one look at him, decided they had to have him, and done something dreadful to his professor to get him. In a way it was perfectly understandable, considering the ill-bred mutts they were stuck with.

"Hi."

The female mutt with the stupid name had walked in. He gave her a withering look.

"Are you all right?" Pogo asked. She'd seen how pitiful he'd looked after his swim but still thought he was kind of cute.

"Am I all right?" Gulliver said stiffly. "What do you think?"

63

"We've all gotten dunked before. It's kind of nice on a hot day, don't you think?"

Gulliver didn't answer.

"Hungry?" she asked.

"You really think I could worry about food at a time like this?"

"Like what?"

"They've done something horrible to my professor!"

"You mean your master?"

"My friend," said Gulliver, who considered the term "master" demeaning. "And traveling companion."

"Traveling companion?"

"We're en route to Paris. Or *were*, till they mugged him and stole my bed and carrying case."

"Oh. Where's your bed?"

"In your house." Under his breath he added, "Or whatever you call that dump."

Curious to see the stolen items, Pogo turned and walked out of the hut. It quickly dawned on Gulliver that the she-mongrel might try to lay claim to his precious possessions, so he hopped off the bed and followed her into the backyard.

"Look, Gully likes Pogo," Consuela commented.

She and the other grown-ups, except for old Mrs. Ponson, were still drinking beer, but they'd turned off the ball game out of respect for Roberto, who was cracking jokes and doing pratfalls on the baked-out grass near the pool with the younger kids seated in a ring around him. Roberto was convinced he was a first-rate clown, for after his very first acting class Ms. Treadle had taken him aside to tell him that he had a lot of natural talent. What she hadn't told him was that she said the exact same thing to all her new students, to keep them coming to class and paying her fees.

"Roberto is a good boy, but he is a ham, I think," old Mrs. Ponson confided to young Mrs. Ponson in an undertone.

As usual, she was right. But he was also the oldest

of the kids, so the younger ones naturally worshipped him, and they laughed and clapped at everything he did.

Following Pogo into the living room on the ground floor, Gulliver was confronted by a very disturbing sight. The other two mutts were sniffing at his bed and carrying case, which had been set on the sofa. Gulliver bolted across the room, flung himself up onto a sofa cushion, and clambered atop the carrying case that should have been heading for Europe with him in it. From this imposing height he did his best to growl.

"Comfy-looking bed," Pudge commented. "I'll have to try it out tonight."

"Over my dead body," Gulliver snarled.

Frankie howled with laughter. "Get him! He thinks he's a Doberman."

"Or a pit bull," Pudge said, snickering.

"What are you, anyhow?" Frankie asked. "A chow?"

"A chow!" Gulliver screamed. "I'm a Lhasa apso!"

"Sounds un-American," Pudge said. "Are you an illegal alien or something?"

"Illegal alien! I was born in Manhattan!"

"Jeez, chill," Pudge advised. "You'll give yourself a heart attack."

"Are you moving in with us?" Frankie asked. "Is that the deal?"

"Moving in!" Gulliver cried. "Here? Are you out of your mind?"

"Well, where's the person you showed up with?"

At that moment the door buzzer gave Gulliver such a start he nearly slipped off the carrying case. But as soon as he caught his balance, his eyes fastened on the front door. Please let it open to reveal his professor!

It didn't open. Carlos shouted something from the backyard, just as when the professor had buzzed. Gulliver turned and looked out a dirty window into the backyard. A man in a red-and-white-striped shirt came into view carrying three flat white boxes, which he set on the table by the boom box. Carlos gave the man some money and opened the top box. Gulliver's heart quaked. Inside the box was a bloody pulp. It all came clear to him. Carlos had hired the man in the striped shirt to kill the professor, and now the man was delivering the remains in these boxes.

For the second time in less than half an hour, Gulliver blacked out.

Wretched

A big wet tongue was slobbering and slavering all over his face. He squeezed his eyes tight and let them spring open in hopes of waking up from this disgusting nightmare.

But he wasn't dreaming. He was lying on the sofa in the Montoyas' sweltering living room. Frankie and Pudge had gotten bored and left, but Pogo's face was hovering over him, her long, dripping tongue dangling out of her mouth.

"Yuck!" he cried, squirming away.

"You're all right?" she said. "You took a header."

He smushed his face into a cushion to wipe off her saliva, then turned and looked out the window.

"They're eating my professor!" he wailed.

"Who?" Pogo asked.

"Those cannibals!"

Pogo trotted off. She returned a few moments later,

giggling in the most inappropriate way imaginable.

"They're having pizza," she said.

"Pizza?"

"People food. Very popular."

"But it's all bloody."

"That's tomato sauce, silly."

Gulliver didn't know whether to believe her or not. But if she was right and the professor hadn't been squashed into a pulpy mass and boxed up, why in the name of dog didn't he come back to get him?

"Let's go watch the stupid clown show," Pogo said.

"Please do," Gulliver said.

He had no intention of budging. Here on the sofa he could guard his possessions and keep watch over the front door in case his professor *was* still alive and came back for him. So while the other dogs frolicked in the breezy backyard, and the human beings stuffed their faces with pizza and birthday cake and beer and lemonade, Gulliver sat in the stifling living room, growing hungrier and hotter and thirstier and more miserable by the minute.

When the daylight finally began to die out, the Montoyas—all except Roberto—invaded the house. Carlos moved Gulliver's bed into a corner and hid the carrying case in a closet and turned on a window fan. Juanita grabbed Gulliver and tried to squeeze the life out of him again, but luckily the girl had a very short attention span and soon abandoned torturing him in favor of fighting over the remote with her brother. Since it was her birthday, Pedro let her have it.

All Gulliver knew about TV was that it was a mindless form of entertainment beneath the dignity of his professor. Now he realized why. The blaring voices and vulgar flashing colors quickly drove him out of the room into the kitchen.

The other dogs were there, all three of their rear ends sticking up in the air as they wolfed their food in true mutt fashion.

"That red bowl's for you, Gully honey," said Consuela, who was sponging off the counter. Even if the red bowl had contained Prime Premium, Gulliver wouldn't have joined a chow line like some stupid farm animal. But the red bowl didn't contain Prime Premium, just cheap dry food.

Out in the backyard it was almost cool, and growing darker by the moment. He sat near the gate, staring forlornly down the narrow passageway his professor had led him up a few hours ago. It seemed like weeks.

His life in Manhattan and Parisian apartments had left him ignorant of crickets, so when their eerie whine started up, it frightened him, and he stole back to Roberto's hut. The door was closed. He scratched. No response.

Anything would be better than the Montoyas' crowded, sweltering apartment, so he climbed the stairs to the second story. The second-floor apartment was hot as well, but pleasantly quiet, since the Ponsons were out, even the old lady. The cat didn't seem to be around either. There was dry cat food in a bowl on the kitchen floor, but the water bowl was empty. Gulliver really was awfully thirsty. He padded back down the stairs to the pool. The plastic walls were too high for him to get a drink.

He ventured back to the Montoyas' pet flap and saw that the kitchen was mercifully free of dogs and people. He went in. But there was just a single communal bowl of water, and disgusting bits of food were suspended in it.

Even more disgusting was the sight that confronted him in the living room: Pudge curled up asleep in his bed, drooling on the lovely chintz! And when Gulliver let

out his most menacing growl, all the uncouth mutt did was crack an eye, chuckle, and doze back off. The other two mutts were taking after-dinner naps on the rug, and the human beings were all staring at the TV.

Gulliver went into Pedro's room. The water in the fish bowl was scummy, the glass filmed with algae. He looked into Juanita's room. The calico cat was standing on the desk chair. She'd managed to open the door of the cage on the desk and had pinned the furry little creature's tail down with a paw. The captive was trying furiously to tug his tail away.

Sorry as Gulliver was feeling for himself, he couldn't help feeling a bit sorry for the little guy as well, so he went over to the chair and growled. The cat shot him a dirty look. Gulliver growled louder and bared his teeth. The cat hissed at him, then hissed "Next time you're cat food" at the caged creature, then scuttled up onto the desktop to an open window. She squeezed out through a loose corner of the screen and vanished into the night.

After a moment a small face peered down from the edge of the desk. The mouth moved, but no sound came out.

"Excuse me?" Gulliver said.

The little mouth moved again, but again to no effect. Gulliver put his front paws up on the chair to get closer. Now he heard something. He cocked an ear and heard the faintest "Yo, thanks, man."

The creature's voice, it seemed, was as small as he was.

"Does the cat do that to you often?" Gulliver asked.

"All the time!" the tiny voice squeaked. "It's the pits, man. She gets in that loose screen. She can open my door. But that's the first time she caught my tail."

The face disappeared, replaced by a scrawny tail with a cut on it.

"Oh, dear," Gulliver said. "What are you, a hamster?"

The face came back. "I'm a gerbil, man. Name's J.C. What about you?"

"A Lhasa apso. Gulliver."

"Well, man, you really saved my skin. Though next time, ten to one . . . She seemed really ticked, didn't she?"

"I suppose," said Gulliver, finding it hard to think of anything besides his thirst. "You wouldn't by any chance have any clean water?"

"It's all yours, man."

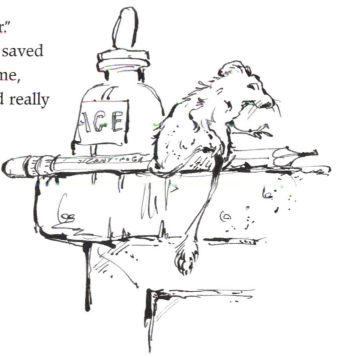

Gulliver backed away and, getting a little running start, hopped up onto the seat of the desk chair. When he put his front paws up on the desk, J.C. was back in his cage, pointing at a water dropper attached to the side of it. It contained only a couple of thimblefuls of water, and there was no way Gulliver could have drunk from it, since the end of the dropper was pointed into the cage.

"Thanks anyway," he sighed, hopping back down.

He checked Carlos and Consuela's room again, but although there was a glass on the bedside table, it was empty. That left the bathroom. The only water he could find there was in the toilet bowl, and he would have preferred dying of thirst to drinking from a toilet.

Parched as he was, Gulliver started spouting tears. They soaked his mustache and dripped onto the bathroom tiles. Poor him! Instead of being pleasantly tranquilized, thirty-five thousand feet above sea level, on his way to Paris to reunite with Chloe, he was about to die of thirst in a tasteless, overcrowded, un-air-conditioned, ground-floor apartment in Queens!

To Sleep . . .

Out in the living room Consuela informed Juanita that it was her bedtime.

"But it's my birthday, Mom! Can't I stay up till nine-thirty like Ped?"

"You've had a long day, sweetie. You're exhausted."

"I am not!"

"Do what your mama says, Nita," Carlos said.

"And brush your teeth," Consuela added.

Scowling, Juanita trudged off to the bathroom. The sight of Gulliver instantly perked her up. She grabbed the weeping dog and fixed her mother's shower cap on his head.

"Look!" she cried, carrying him back to the living room.

Pedro laughed. Pudge lifted his head from Gulliver's bed and sniggered, and Frankie sniggered, too.

"Leave the poor guy alone, it's his first day," Carlos said. "Pudge, get out of there, that's Gully's bed."

After stretching a couple of times, Pudge vacated the bed. But when Juanita set Gulliver down and removed the plastic cap, he dove under Carlos's La-Z-Boy. It was incredibly dusty there. In fact, it was so dusty it occurred to him that he might choke to death and put himself out of his misery. But while he coughed several times, the dust proved no more fatal than the humiliation of a shower cap.

After what seemed like hours, Consuela ordered Pedro off to bed. Ages later, the TV finally quit blaring, and Carlos and Consuela headed for bed themselves, flicking off the lights behind them. Gulliver poked his head out of his dusty prison. The other three dogs were sprawled asleep on the rug in front of the TV. Gulliver wriggled the rest of the way out and crawled over to his bed. It reeked of mutt.

He crept into the kitchen. Chances were the water in the communal bowl was still disgusting, but in the dark you couldn't tell, and he was so thirsty he couldn't hold himself back.

When his thirst was quenched, he stuck out his tongue and plucked a single pellet of dry food from the red bowl. The pellet had a turkey flavor, slightly less horrible than he'd expected. He swallowed it. The next pellet was fish-flavored, truly disgusting, so he spat it into Pudge's bowl. The next, flavored like chicken, was semi-edible.

He ended up finishing off about a quarter of what had been set out for him, and the light supper, though far from "gourmet," left him feeling less suicidal. He went out into the backyard and once again parked himself by the gate. The eerie whining had died away, and the temperature was actually quite pleasant.

All day he'd been disgusted with everything, but now he began to feel a little disgusted with himself.

"What's the matter with you, Gulliver?" he asked himself. "Well-bred dogs don't feel sorry for themselves. He never would have left you in the lurch like this on purpose. If he wasn't in those flat boxes, maybe he's lying in a gutter with a cracked head. Or sick, like that time last winter when he couldn't get out of bed for three days. You have to help him. After all, the hallmark of the well-bred dog is loyalty. "

His coat was already a dusty mess from his La-Z-Boy adventure, so he didn't hesitate to shimmy under the nearby bush and set to work on an escape route under the fence. The ground was very hard, however, and he wasn't used to digging, so he kept having to take breathers. His progress was very slow.

After an hour or so, a puttering sound interrupted him. It stopped. The gate clanged open, then clanged shut. Gulliver squirmed out from under the bush.

Roberto was draping a tarp over a motorbike.

"Hey, guy," he said. "How'd you get so dirty?"

Roberto headed back into his hut but left the door cracked behind him, and Gulliver soon followed him inside. After turning on an oscillating fan, Roberto kicked off his Adidas, tugged off his Multiplex uniform, and ducked into the bathroom for his hairbrush, which had been retired since he'd gotten his buzz cut. When he plunked down on the edge of his bed in his underwear, Gulliver came over and positioned himself between his feet.

Gulliver's tail was soon wagging in spite of itself, for Roberto's brushing technique was even more invigorating than the woman's at Groom-o-rama. When Roberto stopped, Gulliver couldn't help letting out a little moan.

"*Mañana* for more, buddy," Roberto said. "We got a midnight show on Saturdays. I'm totally whipped."

In fact, Gulliver was totally whipped, too. He'd always thought of the day of his first, untranquilized flight to Paris as the most harrowing of his life, but it had been a walk in Washington Square Park compared to being mocked by mutts, drowned half to death, squeezed half to death, choked half to death, starved and parched half to death, then consigned to grueling manual labor.

After brushing his teeth, Roberto climbed into bed. "You can crash here if you want," he said, patting the blanket.

Gulliver looked up longingly but didn't have the energy to make the jump.

"Here you go," Roberto said, grabbing him under the belly and lifting him.

Roberto opened the drawer of his bedside table,

pulled out *The Complete Shakespeare*, opened to one of his favorite speeches, and started declaiming:

> *To die, to sleep—*
> *No more—and by a sleep to say we end*
> *The heartache, and the thousand natural shocks*
> *That flesh is heir to.*

Even if Roberto was a ham, it was nice being read to like this. But by the fifth line of the speech Gulliver's eyes had drooped shut, and by the seventh he was fast asleep.

A Long Journey

When Madame Courgette slipped him a tender medallion of veal, he looked across the café at his professor, who nodded his approval.

"Shall we split it, Chloe?" Gulliver said chivalrously.

"*Oui, merci,*" said Chloe.

They were eating the delectable piece of meat from both ends, her adorable snout drawing ever closer to his, when there was a loud knocking.

"Is Gully in there?"

Gulliver opened his eyes.

"Bug off, Nita," said Roberto, pulling a pillow off his head.

The door to the hut flew open. Disoriented, Gulliver didn't immediately recognize Juanita. Instead of a bathing suit, she had on a frilly white dress and a white ribbon in her hair.

"Gully!" she screeched, rushing up to the foot of the bed.

In the space of a few seconds Gulliver went from a lovely Parisian dreamworld to the wrenching reality of being crushed to this horrid girl's breast.

"Why are you waking me up?" Roberto muttered.

"We're already back from church!"

Blinking at his alarm clock, Roberto saw that he'd slept till noon. He didn't go to Mass with his family, for on his eighteenth birthday he'd announced, rather dramatically, that he didn't believe in God.

Gulliver had never given the question of God much thought, but if he had, he would have been siding with Roberto by the end of his first few days with the Montoyas. What sort of God would take away his wonderful professor and deliver him into the sadistic mitts of screeching Juanita? What sort of God would switch his Prime Premium for crummy dry food, his private bowl of pure water for a communal bowl polluted by dogs with no table manners? What sort of God would deprive him of Manhattan and Paris and dump him in Queens? Replace his operas with reality

82

TV shows, refined companions like Rodney and the lovely Chloe with ill-bred mutts like Pudge and Frankie and Pogo?

Pudge and Frankie mocked and bullied him relentlessly, but in a way he preferred this to Pogo making eyes at him and giving him sponge baths with her tongue. She also insisted on telling him about herself. What possible interest could he have in the origins of her name? (Evidently she'd bounced up and down a lot as a puppy.) What did he care about a trip to the beach where she'd confronted a horseshoe crab? Or the time Roberto had pulled a disgusting thing called a tick out of her neck with needle-nose pliers?

But hard as it was to get away from Pogo, there was someone even harder to escape. It all started his second evening with the Montoyas. Roberto was at work, so the hut was unavailable, and it was pouring rain—Roberto had taken a bus instead of his motorbike—so the backyard was unavailable, too. After forcing down a bit of dinner, Gulliver padded into the Montoyas' living room. His bed was unoccupied, and since the smell of mutt on it had dissipated, he sucked it up and climbed onto the chintz cushion. Despite the blaring TV, he soon drifted off into a pleasant nap—only to be awakened by Juanita's shrill voice.

"J.C.'s gone, Mom!"

"What are you talking about, sweetheart?"

"Come look! His cage is empty!"

While the family was searching the house for the missing gerbil, Gulliver felt a weird tickling on the back of his neck, just above his collar. Then he heard a tiny, squeaky voice:

"Yo, Gully."

"J.C.?" Gulliver whispered. "What are you doing?"

"It was my only chance, man. Tonight that cat was out to snuff me for sure. If you rat me out, they'll put me back inside, and that'll be curtains for little old me."

"Why would I rat you out? Just get off me."

"But if I get off you, the cat'll nab me. No one can see me here. You got such nice long hair on the back of your neck, Gully. It's like silk."

"Flattery will get you nowhere," Gulliver said. "And the name's Gulliver."

He devoted the rest of the evening to trying to get rid of his pesky passenger. Needless to say, he wasn't the sort of dog who rolled over on his back and presented his naked belly to

84

the world. But all his arguments proved useless, and finally, when Roberto got home from work, Gulliver dashed out into the rainy backyard, stopped under the outdoor table, and rolled over in the relatively dry grass. With a squeal, the gerbil squirted away.

Roberto had left the door to the hut ajar. As Gulliver moved toward it, he heard a telltale creak and looked over his shoulder. The cat had slipped out the Ponsons' pet flap and was creeping down the stairs in the rain, eyes fixed on the tiny creature shuddering under the dripping table.

Poor Gulliver. What choice did he have but to trot back and let the gerbil climb aboard?

And, in truth, it could have been worse. The gerbil hardly weighed a thing and was so small that not even Pogo noticed the bump on the back of Gulliver's neck. Two or three times a day the gerbil slipped off to scrounge for food or go to the bathroom, but otherwise he stuck fast to Gulliver. For the first couple of days J.C. yammered on and on about his idol, a wise-guy rat who'd occupied the cage next to his in the pet store where he'd started out. He soon figured out that Gulliver was unimpressed by this lowlife character, however, and quieted down a bit. Gulliver got as used to him as he had to his collar.

Though Juanita was distraught at first, her attention span was too short for a long grieving period. As for the cat, she gave Gulliver darker looks than ever, but whether or not she was aware of his secret rider was impossible to tell.

J.C. aside, there were two things that kept Gulliver's new life from being complete torture. One was Roberto. His hut was a sanctuary from Juanita and the mutts, and Roberto not only let Gulliver sleep on his bed, he often talked to him late at night, trying out speeches and poetry on him and confiding in him about his budding acting career.

"You know, boy, they didn't exactly go ape over my scene last night. *I* thought I rocked, and so did Ms. Treadle. But the rest of the class . . . Think maybe they're jealous of my talent?"

Being spoken to this way by a human being was good for Gulliver's ego. Moreover, he appreciated being brushed after his digging.

This was his real salvation: his nightly digging. Like a husky pulling a mail sled through a blizzard, or a Saint Bernard hiking up an alp to save a stranded hiker, he had the one thing that makes a dog's life worth living: a purpose. He was determined to escape and somehow find and help his professor.

The night finally came—it was his third Wednesday in Queens—when the hole under the fence was deep enough to slip through. But he didn't set out on his adventure then and there. He had no clue how to get to Manhattan from Queens.

He usually slept as long as Roberto, who was a late sleeper, but the next morning Gulliver woke at seven sharp, pushed his way out the hut's door, and dashed across to the ground-floor pet flap. Consuela was standing at the kitchen sink in her bathrobe. Carlos, in his doorman's uniform, was drinking coffee at the kitchen table.

Soon Carlos sighed and said, "Guess I better take off."

"Don't forget about Pedro's game."

"I'll come over as soon as I get home."

Outside the pet flap, Gulliver whispered, "Psst, J.C."

"Mmmm?" J.C. said sleepily.

"Sorry, but this is the end of the line."

"What do you mean, man?"

"I'm going back to Manhattan."

"What's Manhattan?"

"An island. It's the most important borough in New York City."

"I thought Queens was."

"That's because you've never been out of it."

"So . . . I'll just hook a ride and get a load of this Manhattan place."

"But it could be dangerous."

"Sticking around here with *her* is safe?"

"Well, don't say I didn't warn you."

But in fact Gulliver wasn't sorry to have the company, and without the gerbil, who had street smarts despite all his cage time, he wouldn't have gotten far. Thanks to the bangs that fall over their eyes, Lhasa apsos have poor peripheral vision, and if J.C. hadn't poked his head out from under Gulliver's mane on the very first crosswalk and shrieked "Heads up, man!" they would have been flattened by a city bus.

Carlos, several paces ahead, noticed none of the antics behind him. On the next street corner, he picked up his *Daily News*, and on the one after that, he ducked down into the subway. The platform was a steam bath, but the train pulled in before his uniform started getting sweat blotches, and not only was the car air-conditioned, he actually nabbed a seat. He opened to the sports pages and was soon so wrapped up in the box scores of yesterday's ball games that he totally missed the commotion farther down the car.

"Is he with you, lady?" a stout man in coveralls asked.

"Certainly not," said the lady in question, who had on owlish glasses. "Aren't they supposed to be on a leash?"

"Maybe he's going to see his vet in the city," cracked a teenager with cornrows.

"Look at him, he's scared to death," said a kind-looking woman in a nurse's uniform. "He's shaking like a leaf."

"Bet it's a she," said Cornrows. "Check out the girly collar."

"Maybe somebody should take her to the ASPCA," said the woman in the big glasses.

"What is she, anyway?" mused the nurse. "A shih tzu?" "One of them mixes," the man in coveralls said. "Part terrier, part spaniel, something like that." Fortunately for Gulliver, he didn't catch any of this. Even if he'd had more of an ear for human speech, he wouldn't have been able to hear what they were saying over the clacking of the train wheels and the booming of his heart. He'd been terrified on his first flight to Paris, and on his first day with the Montoyas, but nothing like this. Each time the train sped up, the vibrating under his paws made him wish he was back on the trampoline. When the train slowed to a stop, the screech of the brakes made him wish he was with Juanita. And whether the train was moving or stationary, there was such a racket that any reassuring words from J.C. were totally drowned out.

Still, Gulliver never took his eyes off Carlos's scuffed black shoes, and when Carlos finally folded his newspaper and got off the train, Gulliver squeezed out behind him and zigzagged through the sea of legs on the platform, keeping Carlos in sight even as people laughed and pointed at him. It was all very humiliating. But that was forgotten a few minutes later as he followed Carlos down a blissfully familiar walkway in Washington Square.

"That's my building, J.C.!" he said when the tower of One Fifth Avenue loomed into sight.

J.C. peeked out. "Not bad, man. But what's the one way up there?"

Gulliver squinted up Fifth Avenue. "That's the Empire State Building."

"Wow. Ain't seen nothing like that in Queens."

Gulliver grunted smugly.

He stationed himself under one of the laurel bushes by the entrance to his old building.

"What's the plan, Stan?" J.C. asked.

"To get to the seventeenth floor. I have a feeling he's very sick, maybe even dying."

"No offense, but what could *you* do?"

"Well, I don't want to sound full of myself, but I'm sure getting me back would give him a shot in the arm. I'm his best friend."

Several people, some familiar, some not, went in

and out of the building. Each time, Carlos opened the door and then let it swing shut. But eventually a very old man hobbled out on a cane, and while Carlos was helping him into a cab at the curb, Ms. Tavendish, the plump woman from the seventeenth floor, returned from walking her cocker spaniel in Washington Square. She opened the door for herself, and Gulliver dashed in on the spaniel's heels.

"Haven't seen you in a while," the spaniel remarked as they crossed the cool lobby.

"I've been on a little vacation."

"Well, you look good."

"Thank you!" Gulliver said, pleasantly surprised. It must have been Roberto's brushings. "So do you."

Only when he followed them into the elevator did Ms. Tavendish notice him.

"What happened, did Dr. Rattigan go up and leave you behind? That French floozy must be sapping his brain cells."

Ms. Tavendish hadn't been overjoyed by the recent spectacle of Professor Rattigan with Madeline de Crecy on his arm, but she hadn't given up hope. Last night, when she got off the elevator upon coming home from her bridge group, she'd heard arguing through the professor's door. And now here was a chance to do Professor Rattigan a good turn.

She got off at seventeen and, instead of unlocking

her own door, knocked on Professor Rattigan's. To Gulliver's amazement, Madeline de Crecy opened it. At the sight of the dogs she quickly backed away, calling "Oswald!"

Professor Rattigan soon appeared in her place. To Gulliver's double amazement, he looked to be in the pink of health.

"Ms. Tavendish," he said.

"Hello, Dr. Rattigan," Ms. Tavendish said, wondering if they would ever get on a first-name basis. "Look who you left downstairs."

"Gulliver!"

The shock of seeing his professor looking perfectly well was softened by the obvious enthusiasm in his voice. And when

93

his professor swept him up in his arms—something that hadn't happened since he was a puppy—he let out a little yap of pleasure, even as J.C. let out an alarmed squeak.

Instead of carrying Gulliver into their apartment, however, Professor Rattigan called something inside and closed the door.

"My, um, houseguest is allergic to long-haired dogs," he told Ms. Tavendish. "So I farmed this little guy out to Carlos. He must have brought him for a visit."

"Oh, I see," said Ms. Tavendish.

She and her spaniel went into her apartment. Professor Rattigan carried Gulliver into the elevator and pressed L.

"How've you been, boy?" Professor Rattigan said, stroking Gulliver's belly on the ride down. "I've missed you."

In the lobby he set Gulliver on the marble floor and led the way over to Carlos, who was sitting in his chair inside the doors, still absorbed in his *Daily News.*

"So you brought my old friend along," Professor Rattigan said.

Carlos jerked to his feet.

"What in the world . . . ?" he said, astonished. "What's he doing here?"

"You didn't bring him?"

Carlos shook his head emphatically.

"You're pulling my leg, Carlos."

"Swear to God, Dr. Rattigan. He . . . This doesn't make any sense."

Gulliver sat there impatiently while the two men talked. This was supposed to be his big reunion scene with his professor, and now here was Carlos the door-man again. And what was the French lady doing here in New York? Was that why they hadn't flown to Paris? Because she'd suddenly arrived here?

"Your pal doesn't seem so sick," J.C. whispered.

"Perhaps not," Gulliver murmured. "But he's over-joyed to see me."

After talking with Carlos for some time, Professor Rattigan squatted down and scratched Gulliver fondly behind the ears, nearly flushing out the gerbil, who clung to Gulliver's neck tighter than ever but was smart enough not to make a peep. The professor said some-thing, then he stood up and headed for the waiting el-evator. When Gulliver trotted after him, Carlos tried to call him back. Naturally Gulliver ignored this. But when he started to follow his professor into the elevator, his professor held up his hand.

"Sorry, boy. You have to stay here."

Gulliver stared up at the bearded face in bleak bewilderment. Then the steel doors closed.

Numb

Yo, man, you okay?" J.C. whispered.

Gulliver was too devastated to answer. He could have been one of those dog statues in a pet cemetery.

Then up he went into the air. Carlos carried him over to his chair and set him down on his *Daily News,* which he'd spread out on the floor. "I don't know how the heck you got here, Gully," he said. "But you'll just have to stay put till I get off."

After standing a while, Gulliver curled up on the newspaper and shut his eyes. But he was much too confused and upset to sleep.

"Hey, man, I heard a good one back in the pet store where I started out," J.C. said. "Okay. This guinea pig and this white rat and this ferret go into a bar, and the white rat says . . ."

But the joke was lost on Gulliver, as was everything

else that happened that day. Early in the afternoon Professor Rattigan and Madeline de Crecy emerged from the elevator, and the professor said "Hey, boy" as they approached the doors, but Gulliver just pretended to be asleep. He never moved a muscle all day, never slept, never opened his eyes.

Carlos splurged on a cab for the trip back to Queens. When they got home, he located the hole under the fence and filled it in with rocks, then he went off to catch the last couple of innings of Pedro's baseball game. Gulliver, meanwhile, was mobbed by the other three dogs, all dying to know where he'd been. Without a word he turned away and went over to the hut. It was shut up. Roberto must have been at the Multiplex. Gulliver dragged himself into the Montoyas' apartment and crawled under the La-Z-Boy.

It wasn't as dusty as last time—Consuela had vacuumed—but it was still dark and dismal. J.C. dismounted and nibbled on a kernel of popcorn that had rolled under there. After finishing half, he held up the remaining bit.

"Want some?"

Gulliver shook his head.

A while later Pogo poked her snout under the chair. "What you doing?" she asked.

Gulliver didn't answer.

Before long the smell of human food cooking wafted

in from the kitchen. After their dinner the Montoyas took over the living room to watch TV. But not even the awful blaring could drive Gulliver from his hiding place.

During a set of commercials, Juanita got down on her hands and knees, reached in under the chair, grabbed Gulliver by the tail, and dragged him out into the light. "What's the matter with you, Gully?" she said.

"He had quite a day," Carlos said, peering over the La-Z-Boy's arm.

"I still don't believe he got all the way into Manhattan," Consuela said.

"Why would I make it up?" Carlos asked.

"Look at him!" Juanita said, sticking a red barrette onto Gulliver's tail.

Pudge and Frankie looked up from their after-dinner naps and snickered.

"You're not putting that back in your hair now, sweetie," Consuela said.

"It's a present for Gully."

The sitcom came back on, and Juanita hopped onto the sofa. Gulliver dragged himself back under the La-Z-Boy, where J.C. poked his head out through the dog's mane.

"Let me get that thing off you."

The gerbil crawled across Gulliver's back and managed to work the barrette off his tail. But he didn't get so much as a "Thanks."

Carlos waited up for Roberto that night, and when he heard the putt-putt of the motorbike, he went to the back door and peered out through the screen.

"How was work?" he asked, watching Roberto cover the bike with the tarp.

In fact, it was Thursday night, so Roberto had been at his acting class in Manhattan. He and a girl named Moira had done a scene from a play called *The Glass Menagerie*. Afterward the other students had praised Moira to the skies.

"How come you're still up?" Roberto said.

"I wanted to . . . Hey, where's your uniform?"

"Oh. Mine was dirty. I borrowed one at work."

Had Roberto been a better actor, the lie might have sounded more convincing. But Carlos didn't notice.

Roberto came inside and, more as a joke than anything else, got a beer out of the fridge.

"In a year and a half, when you're twenty-one," Carlos said.

Roberto poured himself a glass of apple juice instead and followed his father into the living room.

"You're not going to believe what Gully did," Carlos said, settling in the La-Z-Boy. "He dug a hole under the fence, and today he got into Manhattan. Back to where he used to live."

"No way."

"He did! I was thinking maybe you could write it up and send it in to the *News* as a human interest story."

"Or canine interest," Roberto said, smiling for the first time since his scene. "But how'd he do it?"

"I guess you'll have to ask him."

"Where is he?"

Carlos pointed down. "He's been under there all night."

"Has he eaten?"

"I don't think so."

Roberto got down on his hands and knees and peered under. "Come on out, boy. I want to interview you."

Not even Roberto's voice got through to Gulliver.

Roberto reached and gently tugged him out by a forepaw.

"Hey, boy, sounds to me like we ought to call you Wonderdog."

Roberto carried him into the kitchen and set him down by his red bowl. Gulliver just stood there.

"Not hungry? How about bed, then?"

Roberto said good night to his father and carried Gulliver out to the hut and set him on the foot of the bed. When he climbed into bed himself, Roberto pulled a pad and pen out of the drawer of his bedside table instead of *The Complete Shakespeare*.

After thinking a minute he wrote:

Mysterious Journey
Dog Treks from Queens to Manhattan

He considered this a while and then scrawled:

Canine Commuter
Dog Goes Interborough

"So how'd you do it, boy?" he said, jiggling a foot under the covers.

Gulliver's eyes were open. But although Roberto was grinning at him, all he could see was the elevator doors closing.

The Canine Breast

A famous poet once wrote that "Hope springs eternal in the human breast," but if this holds true for dogs as well, you wouldn't have known it from watching Gulliver over the next couple of days. He didn't eat. He ignored J.C.'s jokes. He ignored Pogo's attempts to start a conversation. He ignored Frankie's and Pudge's wisecracks. He ignored the Ponsons' cat's dirty looks. When Juanita grabbed him, he went limp and waited for the ordeal to be over, then dragged himself under the La-Z-Boy.

It was all such a devastating shock. He'd finally rediscovered his beloved professor—and his professor had completely rejected him. Life as he'd always known it was over. He had nothing left to look forward to beyond this cruddy existence in Queens.

Late that Saturday night Roberto stopped at a deli on his way home from the Multiplex and bought two cans of wet dog food: one beef, one chicken. The household was asleep when he got home, so he used the hand can opener in the kitchen instead of the noisy electric one. He took the bowl of dog food out to his hut, then came back into the house and tugged Gulliver out from under the La-Z-Boy.

"You barely weigh a thing, Gully," he said, carrying the dog across the backyard.

Out in the hut he set Gulliver down in front of the bowl. "I won't tell the other dogs about this if you don't," he said. "Now eat, or I'll spoon it down your throat."

For the past two days Gulliver had been hoping he would starve to death. But starving to death isn't so easy for a healthy dog.

"Smells great," J.C. whispered in his ear.

It wasn't Prime Premium, but J.C. was right. The juicy-looking beef smelled delicious. And Gulliver was ravenous. But eating, he knew, would only prolong the agony of life without his professor.

"I'm a sweaty mess, boy," Roberto said, stripping. "I'm showering before bed."

When Roberto ducked into the bathroom, J.C. dismounted and went straight for the bowl. "Since you don't want to chow down," he said, "mind if I do?"

Here was another defining moment for Gulliver. Was he going to sign off on life and leave the yummy wet food for the gerbil, or was he going to give in and allow himself a little sustenance? What decided him was probably less the smell of the wet food than the fact that someone, even if it wasn't his professor, had cared enough about him to get him this special treat.

"One nibble," he muttered. "But the rest is mine."

The Beach

And so a new chapter began in Gulliver's life. He started eating again. He stopped ignoring everything J.C. said. He quit crawling under the La-Z-Boy. He returned the cat's dirty looks.

This is not to say he forgot the good old days. Now and then Roberto picked up a can of wet food for him, but normally Gulliver was stuck with the same dry food as the other dogs, and J.C. got an earful about the glories of Prime Premium. As bad as the dryness of the food was the unpredictability of Juanita. Some days she hardly noticed him, but other days she would let out a screech and chase him down and nearly squeeze the life out of him. One evening after dinner she squirted whipped cream all over his snout. One Saturday she dressed him up in her bikini.

"Suits you," Frankie said.

"It's darling, Gully," said Pudge.

And, worst of all, Pogo: "You look so cute, I could eat you up!"

Pogo developed a full-blown crush on him. And though being adored is normally considered pleasant, Gulliver couldn't stand her licking his face and telling him how "adorable" he was. He liked to think of himself as handsome, not adorable. Furthermore, she was twice his size, far too large for a girlfriend.

The more Pogo doted on him, the more he pined for Chloe. Chloe was the perfect size, slightly smaller than he was, and she wouldn't have dreamed of trying to lick him. To J.C.'s annoyance, Gulliver took to escaping Pogo's attentions by climbing up to the Ponsons'. In their living room Gulliver perched in an armchair and stared at the photo of the Eiffel Tower, wallowing in sentimental memories of his evenings with Chloe, while the cat, usually sunning herself on the opposite windowsill, hissed menacingly under her breath.

"Ever had snails in garlic butter?" Gulliver mused.

"Yuck," said J.C.

"They're a delicacy. At the café I always got delicacies."

"Well, dude, just in case you missed school that day, cats think gerbils are a delicacy."

But J.C. couldn't keep Gulliver from lingering there, basking in the exquisite ache of separation from the Maltese. Mr. Ponson thought it was the drollest thing in the world. The grinning man in the photo was his brother, who owned the small Parisian bakery in front of which he was posing. Mr. Ponson took a snapshot of Gulliver staring at the photo and sent it off to Paris. "Dear Pierre," he wrote. "You must come for a visit soon and meet your #1 admirer. He stares at your photo every day! Honest, I'm not joking. *Je t'embrasse*, François."

Besides the hours spent reminiscing about Paris in the Ponsons' living room, Gulliver's favorite times were late nights in the hut when Roberto confided in him.

"Well, boy," Roberto said one Thursday night, "either the others have it in for me or I stunk up acting class again. I did this famous soliloquy from *Macbeth*, but afterward the girl in the front row just rolled her eyes . . ."

Or: "Hey, I finished the piece about you traveling to Manhattan and sent it to the *News*. Wouldn't it be great if they took it? I could put the money in my Hollywood fund."

And a few nights later: "The woman at the *News* gave it the thumbs-down, boy. I guess you weren't a big enough deal to get in the paper. But at least she said it was well written and, if I ever have another story, to send it along. That's something, huh?"

After Labor Day, Pedro and Juanita went back to school, and Roberto started classes again at Queens College. But the weather remained summery, and on the third Saturday in September Carlos took the family—except for Roberto, who had to cover a friend's afternoon shift at the Multiplex—to the beach. Carlos borrowed the Sewinskis' SUV and drove everybody, dogs included, to Far Rockaway.

The car trip was an ordeal for Gulliver. Packed into the back of the SUV with the three bigger dogs, he couldn't escape Pudge's digs or Pogo's slobbering. But when they got out and walked onto the boardwalk by the beach, his spirits rose. A beach! His professor had never taken him to the beach, and now, if he was lucky enough to see Chloe again, he would be able to rival her tales of chasing seagulls and running through the backwash.

This beach, however, had no fishing nets spread out

on the sand, only hundreds of beach towels weighted down by human beings. And at first the blaring of boom boxes made it hard to hear the lap of the waves Chloe had described so poetically. But the Montoyas contin-

ued down the boardwalk to a less people-populated, more dog-friendly area where Gulliver could hear the swish of water on sand and smell the salt sea air.

While Carlos set up the umbrella, Pudge and Frankie raced off to investigate a pair of female Irish setters farther down the shore.

"Come on, I'll show you where I saw the horseshoe crab," Pogo said, nudging Gulliver.

"That's okay," Gulliver said. "I'm fine here."

"But it's just past that jetty."

"You go. You can tell me all about it later."

Pogo got the hint and trotted off with a sigh, leaving Gulliver free to perch above the high-tide line and stare out at the ocean. It was bluer than the sky and almost as silky as his coat, shimmering off to the far horizon.

"Yo, man, where are we?" J.C. asked.

"I think France is out there somewhere," Gulliver murmured.

"Oh, jeez. Mooning over that Chloe again?"

While Gulliver lost himself in reveries of his beloved Maltese, Carlos and Consuela set up beach chairs under the umbrella. She opened a magazine, he opened a beer. Meanwhile, Pedro and Juanita started building a sand castle just above the backwash.

The hole from which they got their sand grew deeper and deeper, and once the final fortifications had been added, Juanita had one of her inspirations.

"Let's bury Gully up to his neck! Then Mom can take a picture with just his head poking up!"

Gulliver was salivating over the memory of a piece of coq au vin he'd once shared with Chloe when he was suddenly in Juanita's arms. Before he could squirm out of her grasp, she dumped him in a hole and started packing sand around him. He scrambled out—but Pedro jammed him back in. Before he knew it, he *couldn't* scramble out. All four of his legs were encased in sand.

"Mom, check out Gully!" Juanita said.

"Oh, really, sweetheart," said Consuela. "That's mean."

This didn't stop Juanita. As she patted sand around Gulliver's neck, she felt a lump and let out one of her trademark screeches.

"Mom, look!" She held the gerbil up by his tail. "J.C. was on Gully's neck!"

Gulliver couldn't so much as wiggle a paw, but he

could crane his head back far enough to see J.C. dangling in the air. Was this a bad dream? First they buried him, and now they were torturing his little friend!

"Is that really J.C.?" Consuela said, closing her magazine.

"I don't believe it," said Carlos, sticking his beer bottle in the sand.

Pedro tried to grab J.C. away, but Juanita wouldn't let him go, and poor J.C. was nearly crushed in her fist. Juanita ran to the umbrella.

"Sweet Maria," said Consuela, "it really is him."

"You mean he was hiding in Gully's hair all this time?" said Carlos.

At that moment there was a commotion out in the surf.

"Look!" cried one of the swimmers.

"Rider, rider!" cried another.

"Be careful, kids!" a swimming father yelled. "Dive under it!"

A huge swell was fast approaching the shore. The swimmers who were farther out bobbed over the towering wave like corks. As it turned into a wall of water, the closer-in swimmers dove through it. Then the wall came crashing down, sending a tide of backwash so far up the beach that the Montoyas and others had to grab their towels and books and picnic baskets to keep them from getting soaked.

Till that moment Gulliver's underwater experience had been confined to gentle baths at Groom-o-rama and his one brief dunking in the Montoyas' plastic pool. This was entirely different. The water was salty, not fresh, and he was packed in sand, unable to swim up for air. As the seawater rushed over him, it blinded him, and he was seized with a terrible panic. He tried to bark—and choked on briny water. He struggled with all his might. But all his might wasn't all that much.

Just as his lungs felt the sting of the salt water, the backwash receded, taking with it much of the sand imprisoning him. His front legs were suddenly free. He gagged, coughed, sneezed, then clawed his way onto the soaking sand and tore off as fast as his stubby legs could carry him.

Delivered

As he raced along, Gulliver soon switched from the crowded beach to the shady strip under the boardwalk, where it was cooler and clearer sailing. But after tripping over a stinky fish carcass, he bolted inland onto the streets of Far Rockaway.

Under a hot-dog vendor's cart, he stepped in mustard. As he dashed past a truck playing a jingle, he stepped in a sticky pile of melted strawberry ice cream. Under a parked car he got oil on his sand-caked coat and tail. Then a mean-looking dalmatian caught sight of him and, leaping a fence, started running him down. The chase proceeded through a series of foul mud puddles. As the spotted beast was about to catch up to him, Gulliver leaped through the open door of a FedEx van and dove under the seat.

He crouched there, heart pounding, breathing a mile

a minute, while the dalmatian barked his head off just outside.

Suddenly the beast was yanked away.

"It's them boxes of fancy steaks I got in back, ain't it?" said a short, chubby deliveryman. "Sorry, Rover, they ain't for you."

When the man plunked down in the driver's seat, a spring dug into Gulliver's back, but he swallowed his yelp and scooted over a bit. The man started the engine and drove away. He didn't bother to close the sliding door, but Gulliver was far too traumatized to appreciate the view.

In a few minutes the van stopped and the man left to deliver a package. Gulliver jumped out onto the curb, peered up and down an unfamiliar street, then climbed back to his place under the seat. At least it seemed safe there.

The van's engine had warmed the floorboards, and as his heartbeat slackened, a drowsiness crept over him. He'd been through so much in the last hour that, even though he was driving around an unknown neighborhood in a strange van, his eyelids grew heavy.

When he woke up, it was cooler. The van wasn't moving, the door was closed, the deliveryman's boots were nowhere in sight. Gulliver poked his head out from under the seat. No deliveryman. Gulliver climbed onto the driver's seat and put his front paws up on the steering wheel. It was dusk; he was in a parking lot chock-full of white FedEx vans.

The windows of his were closed. So was the door to the back of the van. He crouched on the seat, quivering, realizing he couldn't get out. Plus, it was getting dark.

For the next couple of hours, tremors of panic ran from his oil-stained tail up his spine to the gerbil-less back of his neck. But once it was good and dark, his stomach began to growl, and he roused himself to search the van.

His dinner was a piece of stale pretzel; dessert, two rock-hard M&Ms.

Afterward, he curled up on the driver's seat and tried to sleep. But a wind was whistling spookily among the parked vans. How he missed having J.C. to talk to! And before long he wasn't just miserably lonely, he was miserably cold as well, for the wind was out of the north, bringing in a cold front.

After a long, cold, and mostly sleepless night, day finally broke. And as the sun rose in the sky, the van gradually grew warmer. But no less lonely. It was Sunday, so no deliveryman arrived.

Gulliver spent most of the day tormenting himself with memories of glorious Sundays of old with his professor, but at dusk hunger forced him to ransack the cab again. This time he came up with half a peanut and a leathery piece of pepperoni. And after this poor excuse for a meal, he had to face a new humiliation. It went against every fiber of his being to soil his own quarters. However, he had no choice but to go off to the corner farthest from the driver's seat and do his business on an old sandwich wrapper.

After another chilly, nearly sleepless night, Monday finally dawned. Before long, doors started banging and engines revved up. Gulliver crept back under the driver's seat just as the side door of the van slid open.

"P.U.!" muttered a man with a walrus mustache. "How the heck . . . ?"

Gulliver remained huddled under the seat while the mustachioed deliveryman cleaned up the mess. Leaving both sliding doors open to air the cab, the man drove off to a depot where he loaded the back of the van with packages.

As he made his rounds, the man left the sliding door on the driver's side open, providing Gulliver with numerous chances to escape. But none of the neighborhoods looked the least bit familiar. During one delivery Gulliver hopped down to grab two french fries out of the gutter, but after gobbling them up, he climbed back under the seat.

Once again the engine heated the van's floorboards. Once again Gulliver grew drowsy and dozed off. So he missed the stop at the tollbooth and the trip through the Midtown Tunnel. But some time after entering Manhattan, the van got caught in a traffic jam. A cabby behind them laid on his horn. Gulliver opened his

119

eyes. He blinked in astonishment. He squeezed his eyes shut again, figuring he must be dreaming. But when he reopened them, nothing had changed. There, visible between two parked Lincoln town cars, barely twenty-five feet away, were the pimply-faced doorman and the tinted-glass door to Rodney's glass tower.

A Reunion

If jigs weren't so unrefined, Gulliver would have danced one. For two solid days nothing remotely good had happened to him, and now, as if by magic, he'd landed on his friend's doorstep!

He darted out from under the driver's seat and escaped the van without the deliveryman even noticing. Under one of the town cars, he found a peppermint Life Saver. It wasn't very satisfying but somehow seemed a good omen. Up on the curb he hid behind a fire hydrant. His nose told him that numerous dogs had used it for their purposes, but it was a good vantage point.

Every minute or so Rodney's doorman opened the door of the glass apartment tower for someone or other, but for a while the only dogs to emerge were a pair of tall, slender Russian wolfhounds leading a tall, slender fashion model. Then half a dozen dogs emerged at once, followed by a young man with an earring like Roberto's. Gulliver, who'd seen dog walkers down-town, always used to stick his snout up at the dogs: poor creatures forced to take their walks in gangs. But as these approached his hydrant, they stuck *their* snouts in the air.

"Look at the bum," said a pug.

"Must be one of them strays," said a bulldog.

"Probably end up in the pound," said a female whip-pet. "Then if nobody wants you, they put you to sleep."

A bum? A stray? Him? And what did that mean, "put you to sleep"? Gulliver rose to his full eleven inches and said:

"Who do you think you're talking to?" The bulldog, not caring for the haughty tone, went for him, nearly yanking the walker off his feet.

"Hey!" the young man cried, pulling the bulldog back.

The doorman came racing over with a broom. "Git!" he cried, batting at Gulliver.

This was a new low: being chased off by a pimply doorman. His self-esteem more bruised than ever, Gulliver crouched under a long white limousine parked farther down the block. From there he could still watch the door to the glass tower, but the chauffeur kept the engine running and the exhaust fumes began to burn Gulliver's eyes and throat.

Just as he was about to abandon his hiding place, out of the glass tower came Rodney, followed by his professor. Gulliver's first impulse was to race over to them. But something told him this might not be a good idea, so he settled for shadowing them up the avenue, creeping along under parked vehicles while they used the sidewalk.

At the first corner they turned left, and halfway up that block they entered a small pocket park. It was hemmed in by buildings on three sides, and at the back was a fenced-in dog run. After releasing Rodney in the run, the professor sat on an unoccupied bench, where he put on reading glasses and started leafing through an art magazine. On another bench a lady

with a blue rinse was feeding pigeons bits of stale bread. On another, two women who looked like twin sisters were reading different sections of the same newspaper. Other than Rodney, the only dogs in the run were a pair of male Highland terriers who looked like twins themselves.

Holly bushes had been planted at the base of the building on the east side of the park, and as Gulliver crept under them, the thorny leaves tore at his coat. But he managed to reach the wire fence that enclosed the dog run.

"Liver and bacon," one terrier was saying.

"Mine was sirloin," Rodney replied. "And this morning he gave me a piece of his sausage."

"Link or patty?" asked the other terrier.

"Link. Quite spicy, but good."

Suddenly Gulliver's mouth was watering. "Rodney!" he hissed.

Rodney looked around in surprise.

"Over here!" Gulliver said, emerging from under a holly bush.

Rodney walked over to the fence, his eyes a-squint under his bushy eyebrows.

"It's me! Gulliver!"

"Good grief, is it really? You look dreadful." Rodney took a step back from the fence. "You smell dreadful, too."

"If you'd been through what I have, you might not smell so wonderful yourself."

"How come you're alone? Where's your professor?"

"Oh, Rodney. You won't believe it. He left me with our doorman in Queens."

"Queens!" Rodney said, aghast.

"Then they took me to the beach and buried me alive."

"Buried you alive?"

"Yes! Then I escaped and spent two days in a prison. Without my gerbil."

"Your gerbil? Have you been eating catnip?"

"It's all the dog's truth! And I've hardly eaten in two days. I'm starving!"

"And look at your coat, it's a disgrace. When were you last at the groomer?"

Gulliver peered around at himself. His coat bore witness to—among other things—sand, oil, strawberry ice cream, mustard, mud puddles, and exhaust fumes.

"The doorman's oldest son brushes me regularly," he said, trying to maintain a bit of dignity. "But the last two days . . . Oh, Rodney, you've got to help me. Would your professor take me in?"

Rodney moved another step backward. "My dear Gulliver, you know that's impossible."

"Why?"

"Because . . . because *I'm* his dog. Why on earth would he want a Lhasa when he already has a pure-bred schnauzer?"

"But we're precious! We're sacred!"

"Maybe to some kooky monk from Tibet. But this is the Upper East Side."

Gulliver's throat was tightening up. "But . . . aren't we friends?"

"Well, certainly. I enjoyed our conversations. And your apartment . . . well, it's not very high up, and it's a bit old-fashioned, but it's spacious and presentable."

What would Rodney say about the ramshackle house in Queens? And even that was lost to Gulliver now.

"Couldn't you get me something to eat?" he said,

trying not to sound like a beggar. "I really am close to starving."

"I wish I could. But what am I supposed to do? Throw a can of Prime Premium out the window—from the forty-eighth floor? Do you have any idea how dangerous that would be? I could get my professor sued."

"Hey, Rodney," called out one of the terriers. "Look who's coming."

A man in a tweed jacket was walking into the park with a female toy poodle who'd clearly just had a French clip.

"Er, excuse me," Rodney said, not wanting Hermione—such was the poodle's name—to catch him associating with a smelly stray.

Of all the shocks Gulliver had had to absorb over the last few weeks, none was more wrenching than watching Rodney turn tail and walk away from him right after he'd pleaded for his help. Gulliver skulked off under the holly bush, his eyes filling with tears as the thorns pricked his soiled coat.

Now he was lost in every sense of the word. He was uptown in Manhattan, but he wasn't quite sure where, since on his previous visit to this neighborhood he'd come in a cab. And even if he'd been able to orient

himself, what good would it do? He couldn't go to One Fifth Avenue. His professor didn't want him.

He left the pocket park and slunk along underneath parked cars, blinking away his tears and thinking of the words of the whippet: "If nobody wants you, they put you to sleep." *Put you to sleep.* How ominous that sounded—and yet how curiously comforting!

Suddenly his ears were assaulted by screeching tires. He'd wandered right out onto an avenue! As he dashed under a bus and made it to the other side, people on the sidewalk yelled at him. Then a construction worker started chasing him.

"I'll help you, doggie," the man cried. "Just stop."

Faint from hunger though he was, Gulliver took off down a side street at a full sprint. At the next avenue he followed a crowd of people across a crosswalk, then bolted down another side street. At the end of the block he stopped to catch his breath and looked back. The construction worker was nowhere in sight. Gulliver looked ahead to a ramp leading up to the towering Fifty-ninth Street Bridge.

He trotted up the ramp onto a pedestrian path running along the northern side of the bridge's lower roadway. He had to dodge a pack of bikers and several skateboarders, but in time he managed to reach the middle of the bridge. He stopped and peered out through crisscrossing girders. Off to his right was

Roosevelt Island. Off to his left, the Upper East Side. He poked his head out between girders. Far below was the turbulent, gleaming river. He thought of Saturday, when the ocean had swept over him. If only he'd just drowned then and there and spared himself all the tortures and humiliations of the last two days!

Gulliver shut his eyes and jumped.

An E-mail Attachment

One morning a couple of weeks later, Carlos was sitting on his stool in the lobby of One Fifth Avenue reading the *Daily News* when the elevator door opened and out strode Professor Rattigan with his briefcase.

Carlos stood uneasily. "Hey, Dr. Rattigan. Haven't seen you in a while."

"I took Madeline to visit my parents in Florida," Professor Rattigan said a bit wearily. "We just got back last night."

"How was it down there?"

"Extremely hot." He rolled his eyes. "She's still recovering. How's Gulliver? Behaving himself?"

"He's quite a dog" was all Carlos said as he opened the door for the professor.

The reason Carlos answered so evasively was that he had no idea if Gulliver was behaving or not. He hadn't seen hide nor hair of him since the dog raced off down the beach three Saturdays ago. He'd checked with the Far Rockaway police, with the local ASPCA, and with the dog pound, but no lost Lhasa apso had been reported. He felt terrible about it, especially for Roberto, who was even more upset than Juanita—perhaps because Juanita had the consolation of getting her gerbil back. Even Pogo seemed upset, moping around with none of her usual bounce. Roberto had made missing-dog flyers and motorbiked over to Far Rockaway and posted them all over the place, but so far no one had called to get the fifty-dollar reward they'd offered for news of Gulliver.

Carlos, who dreaded telling Professor Rattigan that his precious dog was lost or maybe even dead, went home to Queens that night hoping against hope for good news. Instead, there was another missing-animal crisis. Juanita had come home from school to find the Ponsons' cat in her room. The cat had actually opened the door of J.C.'s cage and was groping around inside for the gerbil. After grabbing the cat by the scruff of the neck and lugging the howling thing out to the backyard, Juanita had gone back to her room to close up the cage, only to find it empty. A thorough hunt of the apartment had turned up nothing.

At dinner Juanita milked the loss for all it was worth, twice bursting into tears. She was clearly laying it on thick, but Roberto, off from work that night, couldn't help admiring her natural acting ability. He was genuinely torn up about Gulliver, but when he'd tried to bring tears to his eyes about it, as a sort of acting exercise, he'd failed.

Just as remarkable as Juanita's ability to turn on the waterworks at will was the way she was instantly all sunshine and smiles when old Mrs. Ponson came down with a home-made spice cake by way of apologizing for the cat. Consuela insisted the old woman sit and have a piece of cake with them.

It wasn't long before Mr. Ponson appeared at the back screen door.

"Come on in, François," Carlos said. "Your mom's cake's fantastic."

Mr. Ponson stepped inside but remained standing.

"Sorry about the gerbil," he said. "But on the brighter side, I may have some news about the Lhasa."

"Really?" Roberto said eagerly. "Somebody found him?"

"Well, it's kind of hard to believe. But I just checked my e-mail, and there's one from my brother, Pierre. He claims to have the dog."

"I thought your brother lived in France," Carlos said.

"He does," Mr. Ponson said. "Paris."

"What?" said Roberto. "That's nuts. And how would he know about Gully, anyway?"

"Well, I told you how the dog's always staring at his photo? I sent him a snapshot of it. He says it's the same dog. Same fancy collar."

"That's impossible," said Carlos.

"How on earth could a dog get from Far Rockaway to Paris, France?" Consuela said.

"You never know," said old Mrs. Ponson. "When I was young I never think I go from Martinique to New York City."

"Pierre sent along a digital photo," François said. "Want to see?"

Roberto and Juanita jumped up, their napkins falling to the floor. Nor could Carlos resist following them upstairs to the second-floor apartment.

François's laptop was open on a desk in the master bedroom. When he pulled up the photo attached to his brother's e-mail, Juanita cried, "That's not Gully. He's too skinny!"

Roberto leaned close to the screen. The Lhasa apso in the photo, posed on a metal café chair, was indeed emaciated, and not well-groomed. But around his neck was the salmon-colored collar with the silver and turquoise studs. And though the eyes peering out from under the tangled bangs were awfully sad, he was almost positive they were Gulliver's.

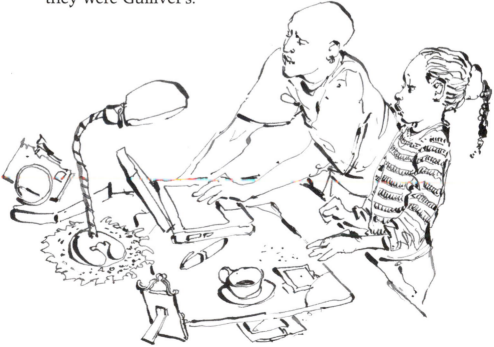

The Seine

Besides a trip to Puerto Rico to meet his dying grandmother, Roberto had never been out of the northeastern United States. But a mere thirty-six hours after seeing the digital photo on Mr. Ponson's laptop he was tossing his knapsack and Gulliver's carrying case into the backseat of a funny taxicab—pale green instead of yellow—at Orly airport in Paris.

"Do you speak English?" he asked as he slid into the backseat.

"Of course," the driver snapped.

Roberto gave him the street address of Monsieur Pierre Ponson, and off they went. From the way the gruff driver weaved in and out of the airport traffic, Roberto figured the meter must speed up along with the tires. Soon they were barreling down a highway that reminded him more of New Jersey than of the Paris he'd seen in movies. But before long the roadway rounded the side of a hill, and there, gleaming in the bright morning sunlight, were the Eiffel Tower and the spires and steeples of the great French capital.

Soon the driver was slaloming down a grand boulevard bordered by trees with mottled, peely bark and kiosks plastered with advertisements for strange-looking products. Cars didn't stick to lanes: driving seemed to be a total free-for-all. Even when the driver turned down a cobbled street far narrower than any in Queens, he managed to swerve around other cars.

The street widened out onto a little square, and the taxi screeched to a halt across from the bakery with the blue-and-white awning—it had the word *boulangerie* on it—the one from the picture in the Ponsons' living room. Roberto counted out some of the foreign currency he'd exchanged dollars for at the airport. He had no idea how much to tip over here, so he gave fifteen percent, which got an honest-to-goodness smile from the surly driver.

After the taxi screeched away, Roberto just stood there a moment on the hosed-down cobblestones, carrying case in one hand, knapsack in the other, eyes fixed on the top of the Eiffel Tower, which was visible over the roof of the building opposite. On the overnight flight he'd dozed off about twenty times, and each time he'd woken up, he'd wondered if he'd done the wrong thing in depleting his Hollywood fund to pay the airfare. But now that he was here, inhaling the mingled odors of freshly baked bread and wet stone, gazing up at the famous tower, he somehow knew he'd done the right thing.

A bell over the door tinkled when he walked into the *boulangerie*. A pretty girl about his age smiled at him from behind a glass case displaying all sorts of delicious-looking breads and pastries. She spoke to him in French.

"Sorry, *je ne parle pas fran-çais*," he said, using his one French phrase. "Is Monsieur Ponson around?"

The girl turned to a door-way screened with hanging strands of colorful beads and called out something in French. Soon Monsieur Ponson emerged through the beads—instantly recognizable from the photo despite the fact that his dark face and hair were consider-ably lightened by a dusting of flour.

He came around the counter grinning and embraced Roberto as if he were a long lost member of the family.

"Bienvenue à Paris," he said. "Welcome to Paris."

The French Mr. Ponson was far thinner than the American one, which was kind of surprising, considering his profession, and he spoke in a lyrical way that was pleasing to the ear. He called Roberto *Robert* (Row-bear).

"Robert, I wish you to meet Felice."

Roberto put down the carrying case and knapsack and offered his hand across the counter. This seemed to take the girl by surprise, but after a moment she reached over and gave his hand a quick shake. Her huge brown eyes, peering out from under clipped brown bangs, had a tinge of purple in them, like Dr. Pepper.

"You must be hungry from your voyage," Mr. Ponson said. "You will have brioche? Croissant?"

138

"Wow, thanks. But . . . is Gully really here?"

Mr. Ponson picked up Roberto's knapsack and led the way to a door in the back of the shop. Roberto grabbed the carrying case and followed the man up a narrow staircase to a sort of garret apartment. The furniture in the living room was pretty modern; on a white formica table, toasters were winging their way across the screen of a laptop. Mr. Ponson motioned to Roberto, who set down the carrying case and followed the man down a little hallway that led to a kitchen. A scrawny Lhasa apso was curled up asleep on the floor by the stove.

"It is him?" Mr. Ponson whispered.

Roberto stared for a few moments, then nodded his head.

"He's exhausted," Mr. Ponson whispered. "The first two days he just sit and shiver, but he finally fall asleep. He choose the warmest place."

Roberto wanted to pick Gulliver up, but the poor dog clearly needed his sleep, so he followed Mr. Ponson back out into the living room.

"How'd you . . . How'd he get here, sir?"

"Pierre."

"Pierre."

"It was Tuesday. On Tuesday morning I always take the Turkish bath." Pierre grinned. "The heat remind me of home, I think. I walk back by the Seine and this dog sits by himself staring down at the water."

"The Seine?"

"The river, just over there. It go through Paris. So this dog look like the one in the picture François send me. And then I see the collar. This unusual collar, no? So I click my tongue, and he look up. He look at me hard. Then when I turn to go, he follow me. So I give him some food, but he don't eat. Like I say, he just sit shivering, mostly. I take a picture and send it to François."

"Could you show me where you found him?"

"Don't you wish to rest after your voyage?"

"Oh, I'll find a youth hostel later. First I—"

"Youth hostel? But you stay here." Pierre opened the door to a small room with a bed in a nook under a dormer window. "It is not deluxe, but just for you," he said.

"Wow, that's . . . thanks." Carlos had given him two hundred dollars spending money, but it wouldn't have gone far if he'd had to rent a room.

"Let me wash, and I show you," Pierre said, setting the knapsack on a chair.

"You can take off now?"

"It is my shop. And I have a very good apprentice."

Pierre soon emerged from the bathroom minus the dusting of flour. On the walk to the river, several people greeted him by name, including an old woman sweeping out the gutter with a broom made of twigs. Soon Roberto had his first look at the Quai. Set up by a long stone wall overlooking the river were stalls offering used books and prints and maps for sale. Pierre led the way toward a low stone bridge, but instead of crossing it, he turned down a set of stone steps that took them to a lower riverbank, where several boats were tied up. Two cabin cruisers, a small barge, and a tourist boat called *L'Esprit de la Seine* with pictures of tourist attractions like Notre Dame Cathedral and the Eiffel Tower painted on the stern. It was by this boat that Pierre stopped.

"The dog was right here," he said. A gnarled-up man in a faded blue Breton fisherman's jacket and a beret was smoking a smelly cigarette on the deck of the tourist boat. When Roberto asked if he spoke English, the man squinted at him and said, "A leeetle, yes."

"Do you know anything about a dog, sir? A Lhasa apso?"

The man shrugged, mystified. Then Pierre said something in French, and the two of them started an animated conversation that made Roberto wonder if he should have taken French instead of Drama as his elective last year. After about five minutes, Pierre thanked the boatman and led Roberto back up the stone steps to the Quai.

"We have a little lunch, yes?" he said.

"Great. But what did he say about Gully?"

Pierre led him down a side street to what was clearly a very popular outdoor café. They squeezed into rickety metal chairs at a small table, and Pierre ordered something called *croques monsieurs* and, to Roberto's delight, a carafe of white wine with *two* glasses. Best of all, the waiter filled both glasses without carding him.

"You know I'm not twenty-one yet," Roberto whispered when the waiter sidled away.

"To your first visit to *la belle France*," Pierre said, clinking glasses.

The wine tasted a bit bitter, but Roberto pretended to like it. "So what did the boat guy say?" he asked.

"He does tours up and down the Seine. He docks in Le Havre—this is the port at the end of the river—and a dog jump off another boat to his deck."

"What kind of other boat?"

"A fishing boat. How you say . . . a trawler. He talk to the crew, they are mostly Dutch, and they say they get the dog from another fishing boat, an American one, way off in the Grand Banks. The Americans say they fish the dog out of garbage, in the water near the Long Island."

After digesting all this, Roberto said, "You think Gully got onto one of those garbage scows?"

"This he did not know. Still, it is quite a history, no?"

A *croque monsieur* turned out to be something like a ham-and-Swiss sandwich, only grilled and better. But Roberto was too excited to pay much attention to his lunch.

"You've got a digital camera, right?" he said.

Pierre nodded.

"And you'd act as a translator for me?"

"I think it is possible."

A plan was taking shape in Roberto's mind. He would interview the boatman and snap a photo of him with Gulliver on the boat. When he got home, he would take a picture of the beach at Far Rockaway where Gulliver had vanished. Then he would write up the story to the best of his ability and send it to the woman at the *Daily News*. And perhaps he could get Pierre to translate the piece into French and interest a Parisian newspaper in it . . .

His eagerness to get started was so plain that Pierre skipped his usual after-lunch espresso. He laughed off Roberto's attempt to pay the bill, and instead of checking on his apprentice when they got back to the shop, he followed Roberto upstairs so he could lend him his digital camera.

Roberto headed straight for the kitchen. No dog was curled up by the stove. He went back and joined Pierre in the living room.

"He's not there," he said.

"Really?"

Pierre clucked his tongue. Gulliver didn't appear.

"Oh, no!" Roberto cried. "Don't tell me I came all this way and now—"

"Was that open before?" Pierre said, pointing at the door of the carrying case.

It hadn't been. Somehow Gulliver must have managed to open it. For when Roberto squatted down and peered inside, there the dog was, curled up inside, fast asleep.

This time Roberto couldn't resist. He reached in and stroked the dog's belly.

"Hey, Gully," he murmured.

Gulliver opened his eyes. For one ecstatic moment he thought the familiar face actually was Roberto's. But then he realized he must be dreaming and closed his eyes again.

"Gully, it's me," Roberto said.

Gulliver reopened his eyes. Whether he was dreaming or not, the hand on his belly was the nicest thing he'd ever felt. He twisted his head around and gave the hand a lick.

The Article

New York *Daily News*
Wednesday, October 27

GULLY, THE TRANSATLANTIC LHASA

BY ROBERTO MONTOYA

THIS PAST JULY the Montoyas of Astoria, Queens, got a new addition to the family: Gully, a six-year-old Lhasa apso. A beautiful purebred, Gully came with an exotic collar studded with silver and turquoise, courtesy of his former owner. After a couple of weeks in his new home, Gully must have started feeling homesick for his former owner, for he made a miraculous solo journey all the way back to his old address in Manhattan. How he accomplished this amazing feat none of the Montoyas could figure out. Gully had dug a hole under the backyard fence, but how he got from Astoria to Washington Square remains a mystery to this day.

But that trip is nothing compared to the one Gully

completed in late September.

His odyssey began on a bright, sunny Saturday a little over a month ago when the Montoya family took him to a beach in Far Rockaway. The two youngest Montoya children decided it would be fun to bury Gully up to his neck in the sand. What they didn't count on was the Atlantic Ocean producing a huge swell. When the wave crashed on the shore, foamy water swept up onto the beach, soaking beach towels and radios and picnic baskets — and nearly drowning the poor Lhasa. When the water receded, the traumatized creature clawed his way to freedom and ran away from his tormentors.

Over the next few weeks, the Montoyas did everything in their power to locate the dog, but their phone calls and missing-dog posters didn't produce any results. Just as they were facing up to the fact that they would never see Gully again, Mr. François Ponson, their upstairs neighbor, brought them an astonishing piece of news.

It so happened that over the summer Gully had taken to spending quite a bit of time in the Ponsons' apartment. He would sit on a chair and stare at a photo of Mr. François Ponson's brother, Mr. Pierre Ponson. In the photo Mr. Pierre Ponson is standing in front of the bakery he owns in Paris, France. Above the bakery, or "boulangerie," the top of the Eiffel Tower is visible. Why was Gully so taken with this photo? Probably because he'd often visited Paris with his former owner. But whatever the reason, the dog's behavior seemed so amusing to Mr. François Ponson that he sent his brother a photo of the dog ogling the photo.

Mr. François Ponson's piece of news was that his brother Pierre had just e-mailed him a photo of Gully from Paris. Mr. Pierre Ponson had recently been walking home and noticed a dog staring into the roiling waters of the river Seine. A dog remarkably similar to the one in the photo his brother had sent him. And wearing the very same exotic, silver-and-turquoise-studded collar.

Indeed, it proved to be the same dog!

And how had Gully found his way across the ocean? Unfortunately, no one will ever know how he managed to get from the beach at Far Rockaway onto a garbage scow. Maybe a scow was docked in Sheepshead Bay and he smelled something good and jumped aboard. However it happened, he was evidently carried far out into the Atlantic and dumped along with the garbage. There, miles from shore, surely on the verge of drowning, the dog was fished out of the water by a passing fishing boat. Later he was transferred to another fishing boat, and this boat eventually docked at the French seaport of Le Havre, where Gully switched to a tourist boat. It is my guess that what attracted him to this third vessel was the painting of the Eiffel Tower on its hull. The tourist boat carried him to Paris, where by a remarkable coincidence he was found by Mr. Pierre Ponson. Mr. Ponson got in touch with his brother in Queens, and in the end, yours truly flew to Paris to bring the amazing, transatlantic Lhasa home. ∎

Accompanying the article were two photos, one of the beach in Far Rockaway where Gully went missing, the other of Mr. Pierre Ponson alongside the one-of-a-kind Lhasa and the boatman who brought him to Paris.

A Longer Journey

Till now the proudest moment of Roberto's life had been when Ms. Treadle told him about his natural acting talent. But that didn't begin to compare to the day his article appeared in the *Daily News.*

His brother and sister were less thrilled about it. "How could you call me a tormentor?" Juanita cried.

But his parents were every bit as proud as Roberto was.

"This'll put him on top of the heap for that Columbia School of Journalism," Carlos observed.

"You know, honey, maybe he could just skip journalism school," said Consuela. "After all, he's already a professional."

It was true: The *Daily News* paid Roberto two hundred and fifty dollars for the piece. This wasn't enough to replenish his Hollywood fund. But then Roberto was beginning to have second thoughts about a movie ca-reer. The truth was, he'd enjoyed writing the article far more than he'd ever enjoyed doing an acting scene. He was particularly pleased with "the traumatized creature clawed his way to freedom" and "the roiling waters of the river Seine."

If Gulliver had been able to read, he would have been impressed as well. Roberto had done a pretty darn good job of piecing together his adventure. But of course he'd missed things. How could Roberto possibly know about his two days in a FedEx van? Or his mi-raculously finding Rodney, only to be utterly spurned by him? Or his leaping off the Fifty-ninth Street Bridge in hopes of putting an end to his misery?

Gulliver had expected to smack into the East River and drown. But when he came to, he was neither sink-ing toward the riverbed nor frolicking in dog heaven. He was lying on his side in a bed of smelly, squishy gar-bage, his already soiled coat now smeared with coffee grounds and what smelled like rancid bean curd. High overhead a full moon was peering down at him pityingly.

Wherever he was, it was as unsteady as that horrid trampoline. He tried to stand but couldn't. It felt as if all his bones were broken, all his muscles torn. His eyes drooped shut.

When they opened again, the full moon was a hazy sun. Now he was able to get to his feet, just. He was very wobbly, and the footing wasn't good, but by taking puppy steps he managed to make his way across a bed of banana and orange peels to a rusty retaining wall. It wasn't high. He planted his front paws on it and looked over.

The wall lurched, and he was nearly thrown overboard into the sea. That was all he could see: sea. Miles and miles of it, wrinkly and blue-green.

Gulliver backed off and curled up on a relatively unsmelly pile of corncobs. He figured he would soon expire of hunger or thirst, though he was curiously unhungry and unthirsty. He was just achy and weary and scared and lonely and ready to have everything over with. He closed his eyes again and drifted off into the jumbled realm between waking and sleeping. As scenes from his past scrolled by, walks in Washington Square and evenings at Le Petit Café, he wondered vaguely what he'd done to deserve to die alone in a heap of garbage out at sea. Had he been too arrogant, too superior? Maybe so . . . Oh, if only J.C. were around! He wouldn't have even minded hearing about his scummy rat friend. Or if only Roberto was there to rub his belly!

A grating grinding broke in on his reverie. He cracked an eye and saw it was twilight. Then the corncobs started shifting beneath him—and with a mixture of horror and relief he understood exactly what was happening. The bottom of the scow was opening, discharging the biodegradable garbage, him included, into the icy sea. The end . . .

And, indeed, the shock of the frigid water sent him into oblivion. But then, little by little, he grew conscious of a horrid smell. Oh, dear dog! Instead of going to heaven, he'd been sent to the other place! Would his miseries never end? Was he now to be tormented for all eternity by the odor he liked least in the world, the stink of fish?

He managed to open his eyes. Doggy hell seemed to be a little cabin with bunk beds and yellow slickers hanging on pegs and a Coleman stove on a counter and a shortwave radio mounted on the wall. He was curled up on a reeking net.

He stood up to try to escape the smell but felt so weak and unsteady he immediately had to sit back down.

"Hey, Dogfish, you're up."

Gulliver turned and gaped. Human beings were allowed in canine hell? For there, lounging on a bunk in a heavy turtleneck sweater, was a man with a shaggier version of his professor's beard.

The man swung his feet down—he was wearing thick wool socks—and padded over. He scooped Gulliver up, then set him down on the teak floor.

"You're a bag of bones, Dogfish." The man took a plate off a table and put it on the floor. "There you go, some nice smoked cod."

Whether he was alive or dead, Gulliver's stomach was definitely growling. But whether alive or dead, he wasn't about to eat fish. He'd eaten dry food, and shared drinking water, and ridden the subway, and stepped in mustard, and spent the night in a van, and begged from Rodney, and jumped off a bridge. But there were things he wouldn't stoop to, and eating fish was one of them.

In the long run, of course, he stooped. It turned out he wasn't dead. He was on a fishing boat bound for the Grand Banks, and the only thing the fishermen offered him was fish. He didn't eat much of it, and he held his breath when he nibbled, but nibble he did.

He ate so little, however, that the fishermen—there were four of them, all from the Carolinas—feared that he might not last the two weeks it would take them to fill their hold with fish. So they passed the anorexic creature off to a crew of fishermen heading back to port.

This second boat, with its full hold, stank even worse than the first. But overall it was a bit of an improvement. For one thing, these fishermen didn't call him Dogfish.

For another, they ate a lot of sausages and gave him
scraps from their plates.

Though the crew was Dutch, they were selling their
catch to a French cannery, in Le Havre, and by the time
they put into port, Gulliver had actually regained a
pound or two. And when he spotted a tourist boat with
an image of the Eiffel Tower on the stern, he regained

the will to live as well. *Chloe!* He would find his darling Maltese and finally settle down with her!

For once, fate smiled on him. He stowed away in the galley of *L'Esprit de la Seine*, where a cook, who prepared sandwiches for the tourists up on deck, let bits of *jambon* (ham) and *boeuf* (beef) and *fromage* (cheese) fall onto the floor. And on a cool gray Monday in October, after two days of feasting, Gulliver arrived in his beloved Paris. The boat even moored on the Left Bank of the Seine, the same side as Le Petit Café!

Above all things he would have liked to head straight for Cheveux de Chien. His once-silken coat was all matted and ratty, and he suspected he didn't smell so great either. But even if he could have located Chloe's groomer, he had no money, so he had to settle for giving himself a Pogo-like sponge bath with his tongue.

156

Daylight was dying when he slipped ashore. He scooted up a flight of stone steps to the boulevard that ran along the Quai. Familiar landmarks were everywhere. In fact, he was just blocks from his July apartment. But it wasn't July. With nightfall it was turning quite chilly, and when he reached Le Petit Café, the tables under the blue-and-white-striped awning were all empty. The line of French doors, always open in the summertime, was closed. The double doors that served as the formal entrance to the café were closed as well.

Gulliver hid under a parked motorcycle and stared longingly at the warm, smoky glow in the café windows. Human diners went in and out, and now and then sweaty-faced kitchen workers slipped outside to cool off or have a smoke, but every time Gulliver made a dash to follow someone inside, he was either too slow or got shooed away. At around ten o'clock it started to drizzle. A man in a black leather jacket and a helmet came out of a nearby apartment building and hopped on the motorcycle and took off, forcing Gulliver to find shelter under a compact car parked directly across from the café. It was actually drier there, but as the rain intensified, the tires of passing vehicles squirted him, and by the time Madame Courgette came out and locked up the café, he was soaked. What with the wet sidewalks, Madame Courgette was carrying Chloe under one arm, and at the sight of the Maltese's pretty face, Gulliver's heart skipped a beat. But he didn't bark. The Rodney experience had shaken his self-confidence — and besides, he knew he must look like a drowned rat.

Madame Courgette and Chloe got into the very car he was crouched under and nearly squashed him with a back tire as they pulled away. He dashed into a doorway and shook himself dry. Once he calmed down, he curled up for warmth, and the memory of Chloe's face lifted his sodden spirits a bit.

At one point in the night a drunk took over the doorstep, forcing him to move. But at least the rain had stopped, and after warming himself a while on a manhole cover, he found another doorstep to curl up on.

By morning, the clouds had blown away, and when the sun peeked over the garrets, the whole neighborhood sparkled. At ten o'clock sharp, the compact car pulled up across the street from the café, and out stepped Madame Courgette. But, strangely, no Chloe. In July, Madame Courgette always brought Chloe along to the café.

From his doorstep Gulliver watched the kitchen staff straggle in to work. The sun warmed things up, and eventually the French doors were all thrown open and a swarthy young man wearing a turban started setting the outdoor tables for the lunch crowd. At a little before noon, Madame Courgette emerged and got into her car and drove off. Ten minutes later, the little car

returned. Out came Madame Courgette, this time followed by Chloe on a leash. Chloe had two brand-new
pink ribbons in her hair. Madame Courgette must have
dropped her off at Cheveux de Chien on her way to
the café. Gulliver opened his mouth to bark a greeting,
but nothing came out. Had he caught laryngitis overnight? But as soon as Madame Courgette and Chloe
were in the café, he tried again and produced a
bark. Just nerves, apparently.

A pair of businessmen in dark suits sat down
at one of the outdoor tables, and a rail-thin,
red-vested waiter who often waited on Professor
Rattigan appeared to take their order. Soon,
Gulliver realized, the café would fill up with
lunchers, so he couldn't dillydally. He scooted
around to the side of the café and ducked inside
through one of the open French doors.

There Chloe sat, at her usual place by
the door to the kitchen, looking even
more bewitching than he remembered.
Madame Courgette was on a stool

at the zinc bar, going through yesterday's receipts, while the bartender was pretending to be busy polishing the cappuccino machine with a cloth. Chloe's eyes widened as Gulliver crept over to her.

"Hi, Chloe," he whispered.

She looked alarmed.

"It's me, Gulliver."

"Gulliver? Truly?"

"Of course it's me."

"But what are you doing here? It isn't the summertime."

"I crossed the ocean just to see you! I missed you so badly."

She wrinkled her adorable nose. "You don't smell very good, you know. And you look horrible."

"Wait till you hear what I've been through!"

"Where's the man with the beard?"

"My professor? He got together with that woman he always eats here with. They're living in his apartment in New York."

"Now I know you're telling stories."

"What do you mean?"

"She was here for dinner just last night. With another man."

"That's impossible. It must have been a look-alike."

"How did you get here from New York City without him?"

160

"We'll need hours for that. But first . . . do you think she would take me to the groomer?"

"Well, I don't know."

Chloe gave a little yap. Madame Courgette looked around and instantly started cursing in French, pointing at Gulliver. The bartender came running around the end of the bar with a mop and chased Gulliver out of the café. Tires screeched. By a whisker he missed being flattened by a French police car.

Gulliver huddled behind two green plastic garbage cans down the block. Frightened and horrified as he was, he made three more attempts to see Chloe that afternoon. However, Madame Courgette had alerted the entire staff to be on the lookout for a mangy dog who wanted to get at her precious Maltese. Gulliver didn't so much as lay eyes on Chloe again.

At the end of his tether, he finally dragged himself back to the tourist boat. But he didn't slip on board to hunt for food. He just sat by the river's edge, staring into the water, wondering how long a process drowning actually was. Then he heard a tongue cluck and looked up to see a man identical to the one in the photo in the Ponsons' apartment in Queens.

Home Sweet Home Again

Roberto wrote his article about Gulliver's adventures on the flight back to New York, and the piece appeared in the *Daily News* a week later. The following night Consuela invited the Ponsons, who'd played such a pivotal role in the story, to join them for Roberto's favorite dinner: barbecued baby back ribs with onion rings and corn on the cob. It was late in the season for fresh corn, but Consuela managed to find some, and though the weather was a bit cold for using the outdoor grill, Carlos decided they could fire it up one last time before putting it away for the winter.

Usually Carlos did the grilling. But as a rule he got home from work at six. Since he still wasn't back when the Ponsons came down at six-thirty, Roberto volunteered to do the honors. It was a Thursday night, which meant he was missing his acting class, but he didn't really mind.

Gulliver kept him company by the grill. Back in the garret apartment in Paris, it had finally dawned on Gulliver that he wasn't dreaming, that Roberto had come all the way across the ocean to find him. There had been no tranquilizer for the flight back, however, and while Gulliver had been through so much over

the past weeks that being stuck in his carrying case in the plane's hold for eight hours didn't seem nearly as terrible as it would have in former times, he'd been so grateful to see Roberto's familiar face by the baggage carousel at JFK that he'd left his side as little as possible since.

When they first got back, Juanita kept grabbing Gulliver and hugging him. And of course Pogo had given him many lickings, and carried on about how much she'd missed him. But he'd been able to sleep out in the hut with Roberto, and three times already Roberto had snuck him wet-food treats. Though none of them, Gulliver had to admit, had smelled as delicious as these baby back ribs.

"Mmmmm," Roberto said as his mother came out with another of his favorites—one of Mrs. Sewinski's homemade kielbasas.

"For appetizers," Consuela said, tossing it on the grill.

The smell of the sausage made Gulliver a bit seasick, taking him back to the Dutch trawler, but he remained by Roberto's side. Roberto was starting to take the food off the grill when Carlos came out the back door.

"Hey, Dad."

"Hey, kiddo. Sorry you got stuck with that."

"No problem. Something wrong?"

His father looked glum. "Well, I know you've gotten

attached to Gully. And now it looks like we'll have to give him up."

"What do you mean?" Roberto said, setting the two-pronged fork on the platter.

"That's what held me up. Dr. Rattigan asked me to come up to his place for a drink. Seems things didn't go so well between him and his lady friend. They had this big blow-up, and now the wedding's off and she's gone back to France. So he misses Gully. He called a car service to bring us out so he could take him back."

"You mean *now*?"

"I didn't know what to say. I mean, it's his dog."

"But he gave him to us! I bet it's because Gully's famous now."

"He hasn't even seen the article. He reads the *Times*."

"So he's in there right now?"

"Yeah. Why don't you take Gully inside, I'll finish that."

Roberto felt like squirreling the dog away in his hut. But of course that would be childish.

"Come on, boy," he said sadly, slapping his thigh as he headed for the back door.

His mother was deep-frying onion rings in the kitchen, but everyone else was packed into the living room: Pedro playing with his Game Boy, Juanita modeling her *Nutcracker* costume for the younger Mrs.

Ponson, the elder Mrs. Ponson stroking the cat in her lap while the cat glared at Pogo and Frankie. Pudge was napping in Gulliver's bed, as was his custom, and on the sofa Mr. Ponson was describing his Parisian brother to Professor Rattigan, who had yesterday's famous *Daily News* in his hands.

"So here's the amazing dog!" Professor Rattigan said. "And the investigative journalist!"

Gulliver stopped at the threshold, stunned to see

his professor. Roberto slouched up and shook the offered hand.

"This is incredible," Professor Rattigan said. "I can't believe he managed to cross the ocean! And you . . . I'm going to reimburse you for your trip, young man."

"Oh, that's all right, sir," Roberto mumbled. "I got to see Paris. And I got the story out of it." He'd also gotten a pen pal. Though Felice from the *boulangerie* had been shy about speaking English, she'd studied it in school.

"Well, you definitely have a letter of recommendation for Columbia, if you want one. Carlos told me you've sort of taken Gulliver under your wing. I really appreciate it."

"He's a cool dog."

"Mm, I've missed him dreadfully. I hope you don't resent my taking him back?"

Though Roberto couldn't help resenting it, he just shrugged.

"But Gully's mine!" Juanita cried.

"He is not," Pedro said.

Carlos, who'd just brought the grilled food into the kitchen, heard this last exchange. He and Consuela appeared above Gulliver in the doorway to the living room.

"Don't worry, Dr. Rattigan," Carlos said. "You can see we've got enough animals on our hands."

"I know you're having a celebration," Professor Rattigan said, "so I'll just—"

"You're most welcome to join us for dinner," said Consuela.

"Why, thank you. But I've got a driver waiting. And I earmarked tonight for reading midterms."

Catching a glimpse of Gulliver out of the corner of his eye, Roberto had a horrible feeling he might do something dumb like start sniffling, so to get things over with as quickly as possible he pulled the carrying case out of the closet.

"Get out of there, Pudge!" he said, booting the big dog out of Gulliver's bed.

Professor Rattigan stooped down and opened the door to the carrying case. "Come on, boy. Time to go home."

All eyes turned to Gulliver. Pogo trotted over to him and started licking his left ear. Instead of squirming away, as he usually did, he sat there and let her. Her moist, warm tongue actually felt comforting.

"Come on, Gulliver," Professor Rattigan said.

Only when the professor stepped toward him did Gulliver move. For the first time in ages, he dove under the La-Z-Boy.

"Will you look at that," said old Mrs. Ponson.

"Gulliver?" Professor Rattigan said. "What are you doing?"

"He likes it under there," Carlos said diplomatically.

Professor Rattigan actually got down on his hands and knees and reached under the chair. The groping hand touched Gulliver's collar, but Gulliver managed to worm away.

"Maybe he wants to stay here," Roberto suggested.

This idea came as a nasty shock to Professor Rattigan. He felt like dragging Gulliver into the carrying case, but instead got to his feet with as much dignity as possible.

"Gully," Carlos said, clapping his hands. "Come out of there, boy."

Gulliver crouched in the dusty shadows, his eyes shifting from the professor's shiny tasseled loafers to Carlos's scuffed doorman's shoes to Roberto's triple-striped Adidas.

Carlos ducked back into the kitchen and cut off a little piece of the kielbasa, which he took out to Professor Rattigan.

"Try that, sir."

"Why, thank you," Professor Rattigan said, taking the greasy bit of sausage dubiously.

He squatted down by the La-Z-Boy and held the sausage out.

"Here you go, Gulliver."

But Gulliver had had more than his fill of sausage on the Dutch boat. And even if the offering had been filet mignon, he wouldn't have budged.

Professor Rattigan's face was red when he stood back up.

"Sorry, guess he's not hungry," Carlos said, taking the bit of sausage back.

"Gully wants to stay with us!" Juanita cried triumphantly.

"He's been through so much," Consuela said, "maybe he's gotten a little skittish."

Pogo lay down by the La-Z-Boy and poked her snout underneath. "You're going to stay with us, aren't you?" she asked.

Gulliver said nothing.

"Yo, Gully," said a tiny voice.

"Excuse me?" Gulliver said.

"Where you been, man?" the tiny voice said.

"J.C.?"

It was none other. The gerbil dropped down out of the chair's springs onto Gulliver's back.

"How'd you get here?" Gulliver asked in amazement.

"After that sucky day at the beach, I ended up back inside. Back in prison, man. Then that hit-man she-cat tried to put me in a sandwich. I was a gnat's eye from being a goner. But I got away, and since then I've been holing up in this dump. Once everybody's conked out at night, I go out and grab a bite. But it ain't much of a life."

Gulliver took in this information. "Your feline friend's here now, you know," he said.

"You think I don't know that? I could smell her a mile away. So, dude, what you been up to since the beach?"

"It's kind of a long story. How about I tell you later?"

"That mean we're a team again?"

Looking out at the tasseled loafers, Gulliver thought how he'd dug under the fence and braved a packed subway to find the professor because loyalty is the hallmark of the well-bred dog. Shifting his eyes to the scuffed black shoes, he thought with shame of how he'd once thought of Carlos as "only" a doorman. Then he looked at the Adidas, and he was back in the carrying case in Pierre Ponson's flat in Paris, the familiar hand stroking his belly, the familiar handsome boy with the close-shaved head grinning in at him.

"I guess we could give it a trial run," he said.

Gulliver had never made it to Cheveux de Chien in Paris, and he hadn't been to Groom-o-rama since returning to this side of the Atlantic. But Roberto had given him several good brushings, so his mane was fairly silky, and J.C. was only too happy to nestle into it.

Professor Rattigan, meanwhile, was feeling even

more stunned than after his first big fight with Madeline de Crecy. But what could he do? He could hardly force Gulliver to come with him. His only option was to apologize for barging in on the celebration and say his good nights.

"I'm really sorry, Dr. Rattigan," Carlos said.

"It was Gulliver's choice, not yours," he said, trying not to sound bitter. He turned to the boy who'd flown to France to fetch Gulliver back and forced a friendly smile onto his face. "As for that letter of recommendation, young man, it's still yours if you want it."

"Thanks, Dr. Rattigan," Roberto said.

About a minute after the tasseled loafers disappeared out the front door, Gulliver slithered out from under the La-Z-Boy. The cat hissed, smelling J.C., but the human beings all applauded, as if Gulliver were taking a curtain call at the end of a brilliant performance. Even Pudge and Frankie growled their approval. As for Pogo, she came straight for him. Gulliver ducked behind Roberto to avoid another licking.

Roberto scooped him up and gave him a hug. "You're the best, Gully," he whispered, "you know that?"

The elder Mrs. Ponson grinned at them. "Look like famous transatlantic dog settle down in Queens," she said.

It really was remarkable how rarely the old woman was wrong.